THE DEATH
OF
BERNADETTE
LEFTHAND

THE DEATH OF BERNADETTE LEFTHAND

A NOVEL

Ron Querry

R·E·D
CRANE
BOOKS

SANTA FE

For Elaine

First Edition
Manufactured in the United States of America
Series format by Paulette Livers Lambert
Design by Jim Mafchir
Cover painting and text drawings by Gregory Truett Smith

Library of Congress Cataloging-in-Publication Data

Querry, Ronald B. (Ronald Burns)
    The death of Bernadette Lefthand / Ron Querry. — 1st ed.
        p.   cm.
    ISBN 1-878610-25-2 (cloth)—ISBN 1-878610-29-5 (paper)
    1. Jicarilla Indians—Fiction.   2. Navajo Indians—Fiction.   I. Title.
PS3567.U283D4   1993
813'.54—dc20   92-53886
                                                                      CIP

Red Crane Books
826 Camino de Monte Rey
Santa Fe, New Mexico 87501

Author's Note

The reader should be aware that there are no real people in this book: the characters portrayed and the names ascribed to those characters are entirely imaginary. At the same time, however, many of the events and the settings are genuine: Gallup and Dulce, Taos Pueblo, the trading post at Piñon, Canyon de Chelly, Shongopovi Village at Second Mesa—all are described as nearly as the author can recall having known them. And the same may be said of the powwow at Taos Pueblo gym and the ninety-nine *Tasapkachinas* on the dusty little plaza at old Shongopovi.

The reader should also be aware that among Navajo people there are few today who doubt the existence of witches. Indeed, accounts of "witchery" not unlike those depicted in this novel may be found throughout the anthropological and ethnological literature dealing with the Navajo.

One of man's peculiarities is that he requires "reasons" for the occurrences of events. One of the manifest "functions" of belief in witchcraft is that such belief supplies answers to questions that would otherwise be perplexing —and because perplexing, disturbing.

—Clyde Kluckhohn
Navaho Witchcraft (1944)

Gracie

I'm just barely sixteen years old, but sometimes I feel a whole lot older than that.

You know how sometimes a person can get to feelin' like their life's already just about over with? Or worse yet, like they ain't even here anymore?

Well, that's how I feel a lot of the time . . . at least ever since Bernadette died.

It causes my heart to ache, but every day I can't help but think about that morning when those cops came and knocked on our door before my Daddy had even finished getting ready to go to church to tell him that they had some bad news.

"Eddie," they said. "There's been a killing last night, and it was your Bernadette who got killed."

Just like that. "It was Bernadette that got killed," they said.

And then, "We're looking for Anderson George, Eddie. Didn't nobody answer the door at their place and people are sayin' that he was real drunk and mean-acting over at the powwow last night. We need to talk to him."

Then I heard Daddy ask them did Anderson George go after whoever killed Bernadette, but they just said they wanted to talk with him.

Even now I can still remember how I felt real confused

and sick to my stomach and dizzy, and I guess Daddy must have looked pretty poor too, because those cops told him to sit down and to drink some coffee or something. And then after that I don't really remember too much of what all was going on for awhile.

When those cops came I was cooking out in the kitchen and I heard all this talk going on and went into the living room where they were. Daddy looked very old all of a sudden, and his face looked kinda gray.

"Your sister got killed," he said to me real soft-like. "It wasn't a car wreck, but she still got killed."

I guess he wasn't sure if I heard him right or not, because when I tried to say something I just made this kind of funny little noise in my throat and then turned around and went back into the kitchen. And then in a few minutes, when the cops told Daddy that they would talk to him some more later on and went away, he came into the kitchen and I was standing there cutting up potatoes into some stew that was going to be for our dinner that night.

"I said that Bernadette is dead."

I didn't even look over at him, but just kept right on cuttin' potatoes to put in the stew.

"Can't you hear me?"

"I know," I said. But I said it real low, almost like it was a whisper. It was like I couldn't talk any louder, though, even if I wanted to. "Where is she now?"

"I didn't think to ask them," he said. "I better go in the truck and find her."

"You bring her home," I said. "Just bring her home."

And then when he put on his jacket and started to go out the door, I remember I started to cry real hard. And I guess he must have heard me and got worried or something, 'cause he came right back in the house and told me to get my coat on and come with him. Now that I think about it, I think that probably he was just scared and wanted me to help keep him company.

I don't know why, but we drove straight over to the health services clinic.

The cops had said that Bernadette was already dead, so it figures they wouldn't have taken her there, but probably to the undertaker's place out east of town instead. But I don't think Daddy could make himself drive to no undertaker's to see if Bernadette was there, so we went to the IHS clinic which is in a neat, white building with green trim. Actually, it's one of the nicest looking buildings in town, mainly because it's not built like most things around here—out of government-issue green tin. This clinic is built out of wood. Except there's a big ugly orange and white tower out in back of the building, but that's where the antenna for the ambulance radio is mounted and I guess that has to be real tall for the radio signal to work good.

When we got there and went in, a woman was sitting at the desk just inside the door next to where you wait afternoons to get screened by the public health nurse to see if you're serious enough to see the doctor who drives over from Farmington. She was reading a magazine that had a picture of a smiling blond-haired girl on the cover. This wasn't one of the regular nurses I don't think, she was just a woman who filled in on Sundays to earn some extra money. I think it must have been an old magazine, because somebody had taken a ballpoint pen and blacked out a couple of the cover-girl's teeth so she looked ugly. The woman was eating sunflower seeds and there was a pretty big pile of empty shells there on the desk. I noticed that there was some empty shells scattered around on the floor by her feet, too. When she saw us she just barely glanced up before she went back to cracking seeds and whatever it was she was looking at in that magazine.

"I'm looking for my daughter." My father's voice didn't sound normal when he talked to the woman—I guess you could say it sounded kinda shaky. "The police told me that she got killed, but I didn't remember to find out what they did with her."

The woman put down her magazine real fast and stood up. I could tell that hearing him say that had made her nervous by the way she started around the desk toward where we were standing and then just sort of backed away and looked helpless, like she wished somebody in charge would come out so that she wouldn't have to deal with this kind of business.

"Oh my," she said. "Was there a wreck? I didn't hear about any wrecks last night."

She began to shuffle through some papers on the desk. "I'm sure they must have gone to Farmington, though," she said. "The ambulance wouldn't bring anyone here if it was serious, this is just a health clinic, you know. What was the patient's name, sir?"

I could see that this woman's hands were shaking as she fumbled with the papers. I can remember that she had real red hair—not real-*looking*, just real *red*.

"*Bernadette*," he told her. "Bernadette George is my daughter's name."

"No. . . . No, I don't see that we've had anyone by that name here," the woman said. "If it was the tribal police that called you maybe you should check with them, Mr. George."

"My name is Edwin Lefthand," he told her. "Not George. My daughter is married to Anderson George. The cops came to my house a little while ago," he said. "They told me Bernadette was killed, but it wasn't in no car wreck."

My Daddy's voice sounded funny to me. "We forgot to find out what they did with her," he told the woman.

"And we got to get her and take her home."

Looking back, I can see now that he really was just so terrible scared. You know, it was like he could hear himself, and he was talking, but it sounded real far away . . . like it wasn't even him talking . . . like it was somebody else. I remember wonderin' at the time if he sounded far away to that red-haired woman, too.

I guess maybe he did sound funny to her. Because right then she got to looking real sad. Not just kinda nervous like she did before, but really sad in the way she looked at us. I thought she was maybe going to cry and I hoped that she wouldn't because Daddy don't like seeing nobody cry and I'd already not helped things much by breaking down on him, and I didn't know what he'd do if this woman he didn't even know was to start.

"I'm so very sorry Mr. Lefthand," she said. "I can call over to the tribal administration office for you if you'd like me to . . . I don't know what else to do. Your daughter isn't here."

"Jesus, Eddie—you don't want to see her. She's messed up pretty bad, and Bernadette was such a pretty girl. Maybe you ought to go on home with Gracie until things settle down and you get yourself calmed down."

It was John Archuleta who was talking to Daddy and me. And we were standing in the office of the Jicarilla Tribal Police headquarters. Daddy'd been friends with John Archuleta ever since he first came to live in Dulce— back before John even got a job as a tribal policeman, when he still just ran cattle with his two brothers down by Stinking Lake. And now he was the Deputy Chief of the force. I noticed that John looked nervous, too.

"I *am* calmed down, John," Daddy told him. "I just got to take her home, now. And where's Anderson George? Did you find him yet? Somebody's got to tell him."

I could hear the two-way radio crackling in the outer office—where the other policemen sat and drank coffee when they weren't out checking on things. I never could understand what anybody was saying on those radios—it always sounded like just a lot of static to me.

"Not yet, Eddie." John Archuleta put out his cigarette. I noticed that he still wasn't looking at my Daddy's eyes. It was like he was embarrassed to look right at him.

"You should know that some of the people we've talked to who were over at the dance last night said that Anderson was drunk and acting mean to Bernadette, Eddie. We're lookin' into the possibility that maybe Anderson might even have been the one who did this to her.

"How about I drive you and Gracie to the house, Eddie?" Now his voice sounded sad. "I can drive you over there and have one of the guys follow us in your truck. You ought to be at home with Gracie."

"But what about Bernadette?" I asked. "Where is she now?"

"I told them to take her over to the big hospital in Farmington, Gracie. There will have to be some tests and the medical examiner will have to look at the body. When there's been a murder there are procedures . . . rules that we have to follow. You got to understand."

Murder. I felt sick and dizzy and confused again. That was the first time that word had come into my mind. He was saying that my sister Bernadette had been murdered—and it seemed like he was saying that he thought it was her husband who murdered her. I remember thinking then that there must be some big mistake . . . like maybe it wasn't even Bernadette that they took over to Farmington, after all. And even if it was Bernadette, it couldn't have been Anderson that hurt her—Anderson wouldn't never have done anything bad to hurt Bernadette . . . she told me that herself.

That's what I thought then, anyway.

▼▼▼

I don't know exactly why, and maybe it was just a coincidence, but for some reason I get a funny feeling that a lot of the trouble might have started back about the same time that white woman Starr Stubbs came around and started making over Bernadette and acting all buddy-buddy with her.

I guess it was pretty natural that she'd choose Bernadette to chum around with, though. Everybody said my sister was the prettiest and smartest woman on the whole reservation. And even after she had the baby she was just real beautiful, and you know that's the time when a lot of the women around here get real fat and stop fixin' themselves up, and all.

Of course, I ain't never had no baby—least ways not one of my own—but I'm fat anyway. Bernadette always said I wasn't fat, that I was just chubby and that I'd grow out of it. But of course I knew better . . . that's just the way she was—always saying nice things to try and make you feel good about yourself. I never did have nice smooth skin like Bernadette either, and my teeth aren't straight and even. I figure it must have always been sort of hard for our father—you know, to have had two daughters who looked so different. Bernadette always having been just the prettiest thing you ever saw . . . and me, I guess you could say I'm just plain, is what I am.

Anyway, I say Bernadette *was* the prettiest, but of course that's just because she's dead now. She still would be the prettiest if that bastard Anderson hadn't killed her that night when he'd been drinkin' too much out at that powwow and he got ugly drunk and mean and cut her up something awful with that big knife. But he didn't hurt the baby, at least. And that's something to be thankful for. Only I just wish he hadn't hurt Bernadette, either. I miss her a lot. I mean, it's not like I don't love taking care of that baby. I just wish sometimes that Bernadette was still here to be its mother instead of me.

Bernadette was the best dancer, you know.

She had won a lot of the contests at the bigger doin's over at Gallup and in Albuquerque and even back at the big Red Earth gathering in Oklahoma City. And you can bet she had won herself money at some of those pow-wows, too, and I mean lots of money. Especially back before she married Anderson George, back when she did the fancy shawl dance and her feet practically flew above the ground—I mean, those blue and white beaded moccasins she got from some Utes up in Colorado just didn't ever even seem to touch the earth.

I remember those moccasins were made of soft deer-skin and had very intricate patterns sewn onto them in these little tiny beads. It's hard for me to imagine how long and hard somebody must have worked just sewing those beads on. I can tell you I've seen moccasins that weren't anywhere near that fine and fancy for sale at pow-wows for a lot more money than most people could afford to pay. And the thing is, Bernadette got them as a present during a give-away one time when she'd been invited to be the head lady dancer up there around Durango. Those moccasins were just a real special treasure to my sister and she only wore them on very special occasions.

She was gonna give them to me. But it didn't work out.

Anyway, everybody always watched Bernadette when she danced—watched her real hushed and quiet like they didn't want to breathe and maybe cause a feather to fall out of her hair and disgrace her in front of all those peo-ple from other tribes. And it got to be where it was al-

most like it wasn't an honor to win a contest if
Bernadette wasn't there. Oh sure, a lot of those girls
would brag that they were so hot that day that Bernadette
Lefthand couldn't even have beat them if she *was* there.
But I figure they really knew better. I remember that
summer before she graduated high school she let me help
her make her first jingle dress—I swear, you could hear
her coming a mile away and know it was her. Like I said, I
miss her a lot.

Bernadette was four years older than me. I must've
been about thirteen when she met Anderson George at
boarding school down in Santa Fe. Him and his brother
Tom were just about the prettiest Indian boys at that
school, everybody said so, so it figures that's who
Bernadette would take up with. And they weren't built all
chunky and square like lots of Indian guys are either. They
were tall and slim and handsome and always wore those
black cowboy hats with silver and beadwork bands over
their shiny black hair that they didn't cut off but instead
let hang straight down their backs. They were, I think, a
year apart in age, but they were in the same class at
school. Some people said that they were like twins—that
they should have been twins because they went everywhere together and seemed always to know what the
other one was thinking before anybody else did. They
looked out for each other, too, those two did. And didn't
nobody push one around or say anything smart alec unless
he wanted to deal with the two of them at once. Some
people used to wonder how come it was that Bernadette
went with Anderson instead of with Tom. Me, I never saw
much difference between the two, at least not back then,
but Bernadette said that it was because Anderson was not
as loud actin' as his brother and that he had straighter
teeth—she told me that Tom George had crooked and

broken teeth on account of he got stepped on by a horse over at his grandmother's place near Chinle. Maybe that was so, that it was mainly because of his teeth that she favored Anderson, but then maybe she was just putting me on . . . she used to do that, tease me sometimes because she said I had a big crush on Anderson George. And maybe that was so too. But I don't have no crush on that Anderson George now. Anyhow, I never got a clear look at Tom George's teeth that I can remember because he never let you see them and if he was going to smile or laugh or something he had this way of putting his hand over his mouth. It was a habit I figure he had gotten into to hide his teeth.

I remember back when they were first going together, how Bernadette and Anderson used to go to rodeos and powwows all the time. The thing was, Tom used to go along, too. Thinking back, I guess maybe it was really Bernadette who was the one that went along. Oh, it never was a problem—least ways, my sister never complained that Tom was always around. It was like if she wanted to see Anderson, she might as well count on Tom being there, too. Anyway, Anderson was a halfway decent saddlebronc rider at the high school-level, all-Indian rodeos. I say halfway decent so you'll understand that he spent a lot of time picking himself up out of the dirt, and not just being a hero and staying on for the full eight seconds or however long it is that makes a ride count toward prize money. Which is probably one reason that he wasn't ever much of a dancer at the powwows—which you might think he would be since Bernadette was so good—the fact was he was too stove up to dance. That, and also there's this thing about most Navajos not really taking much to the powwow scene—at least not like Plains Indian people and Pueblos do. Navajos have their own kind of get-togethers that they call a Song and Dance . . . but it's different from a powwow. To be honest about it, lots of the Pueblo people don't even like Navajos—and Taos don't, especially. They say that in the Taos language the words they use for talking about Navajos mean that they eat sheep and look awful and are dirty—but I think that's mainly just the old people who still think like that. It just always seemed like everybody overlooked their old disagreements and hatreds whenever it came to Anderson and Tom George—I figure it was on account of them having went to school over in Santa Fe and having spent a lot of time mingling and getting along with all those guys from different tribes. But anyhow, those two boys were singers instead of dancers—Tom always joked that that way Anderson got to sit down at the powwows and sing and play the drum and rest the bruises he got from getting bucked off at the rodeos.

After they graduated from high school, those guys got jobs in the oil and gas fields up around Farmington. I guess it was pretty good money, anyway it seemed like money wasn't a real big problem whenever Anderson and Tom George were around. They went in together and bought a new pickup in Farmington. A black and silver GMC with a "Custer Had It Coming" bumper sticker and a fiberglass camper shell where Anderson could carry his saddle rigging to the rodeos and not have to worry too much if it rained. And they could sleep in the back if they were at a powwow or a rodeo a long way from home. I remember I always admired that pickup truck. Those boys were proud of that truck and always kept it washed—not like most of the guys around here. It was just real pretty.

I'll tell you one thing about Anderson George, though. Even though it's true he might not have been much when it came to dancing traditional and all, still I can tell you for sure there was one kinda dance he could do like nobody I ever saw.

I remember the first time I ever saw him do it, it was at Taos at a powwow in the Day School gym down there. Like I said, some of the people there don't think too much of Navajos—the older people especially—but there never was any kind of trouble that I heard about and I think they liked Anderson and Tom okay since Bernadette did. And you know, everybody loved Bernadette.

Anyway, as I remember it there was four or maybe five drums there that night and like usual, quite a few dancers from here at Dulce had showed up. Me and Bernadette had gone down there in our Daddy's Ford pickup because we knew that Anderson and Tom George was gonna be there. And besides, those Taos powwows were usually pretty good and we knew a lot of the folks there since it was where our Daddy's people were from. The announcer was this guy who was a Lakota Sioux, I think, from up in one of those Dakotas—I don't remember if it was North or South. I'd seen him around some and he was pretty funny what with his joke-tellin' and stuff, and right after one big intertribal dance he asked everybody if they were ready for some real fun and of course we were.

He said that he was going to put a five-dollar bill out in the middle of the floor and that while the Salt River Drum played, the men dancers who thought they were good enough and limber enough could one at a time dance around that money and then try to pick it up in their teeth. And in case that wasn't hard enough to do, they also couldn't let their hands or knees or butts or anything but their feet touch the floor or else they'd be disqualified and have to go sit down. Well, you could see several of the fancydancers starting to limber up and bend over like they figured they would just prance out there and pick up five dollars which would maybe buy them a couple of Frito pies and maybe some coffee at the next break. But then Harrison Morning Gun, one of the head singers from the host drum, walked out and picked up the five and told everybody that he figured it was a safe bet that these puny guys couldn't pick up anything off the floor with their teeth and that he was going to put down a twenty-dollar bill if after all the dancers failed the singers could try!

Boy howdy, I can tell you that there was a lot of laughing and clapping and drum-beating when he said that. Twenty dollars is a lot of money, even though Bernadette told me that one time in Oklahoma she was at a big doin's where they had a *hundred*-dollar bill on the floor! Why, I've never even *seen* a hundred-dollar bill. I figure maybe Bernadette was just putting me on to act smart since she'd been to Oklahoma and she knew I never had.

Anyway, then the Salt River Drum started their song and about half a dozen of the dancers went out and started to dance in a circle around that twenty. You could see that those guys were all watching each other to see who would be first to try for the money and of course the host dancers from Taos couldn't really go first because that wouldn't be polite. So finally this guy from over at Jemez who also happened to be the Headman Dancer at this particular powwow moved in and did some fancy steps and then kind of did the splits down real low. But then when he tried to lean over frontwards from the splits toward the twenty, he didn't even get close before his hands went down on the floor to keep him from falling over. Everybody applauded and cheered him on but he got disqualified. Still, he was grinning when he went over to the side to sit and watch the others try.

As it turned out, that guy from Jemez was really pretty good because none of the other dancers did much better, except for this one young kid who hadn't I guess understood the rules and just walked out and right away got down on his knees and the announcer had to come running over and grab ahold of him so he wouldn't get the money. We all had a big laugh at that.

Once all the dancers were disqualified, the announcer started trying to get some of the singers to try. Finally one young guy got up and tried, but he really just made kind of a feeble attempt at the money to show that he was a good sport, I think, because he didn't do very good and went right back to his chair at his drum. Then an older fellow from Harrison Morning Gun's drum came out to the center and I figured that he probably was gonna get the money because he was in on some secret or trick, it being Morning Gun's money, and all. But he slipped right off the bat and put his hand down on the floor to keep from falling and busting his butt and then laughed real big and went back to the sidelines shaking his head.

It looked like there wasn't no other takers and I think Harrison Morning Gun was fixing to come out and claim his twenty when me and Bernadette noticed Anderson George stand up. He wasn't wearing his regular black cowboy hat this particular night, but instead he was wearing a baseball style gimme-cap he'd got from some feed-store over in Shiprock and had his hair tied back in a ponytail with a piece of yarn. So when he turned his hat around backwards on his head so that the visor was sticking out over the back of his neck, we knew for sure he was gonna try for that money.

Anderson started doin' a little shuffle-step right there at his chair and then he danced slowly out across that gym real cocky-like toward where that twenty-dollar bill was lying out there on the floor. Lord, you could just tell by how cocky he was acting that he knew he was just about the prettiest boy there that night and that there were a whole lot of Indian girls with black, shiny eyes looking at him dance. And he must have known that Bernadette was looking at him, too. And of course *I* was looking at him, and even now, just thinking about it, I can't hardly get my breath.

And I can remember looking over and seeing Tom George sitting there at his place at the drum and watching. And how he looked so cool and calm and collected and yet you could tell that he wanted his brother to get that money—and not because he needed twenty dollars, but because he wanted everybody to see that those George boys were the best in everything. And he was watching and quietly tappin' his big drumstick on the edge of the drum in time with the Salt River guys across the way.

And Anderson was dancing better than I ever saw him dance. He'd shuffle and then skip and turn and bend low from his waist and do a half-spin and turn his head real fast-like so that that black ponytail of his swished around and then he'd stand up straight and tall so everyone could see that he was Anderson George, the singer. And like I already told you, he was tall for an Indian, and drop-dead handsome.

Oh, and I wish you could have seen Bernadette, too. Her eyes were just glued on Anderson. And you could see that she knew that some of the other girls sitting around the gym were sneaking looks toward where we were sitting because they knew that Bernadette was Anderson's girlfriend. And Bernadette had her hands up to her face to cover up, I think, that her cheeks were burning and starting to turn red from watching Anderson dance and knowing that he was fixing to try for that twenty-dollar bill and praying that he wouldn't mess up but figuring that he would since even the regular dancers hadn't even come close and that while he might be a pretty good saddle-bronc rider most of the time, he wasn't really much of a dancer to speak of.

The Salt River Drum was beating a steady, heavy beat

and Anderson George was sure enough taking his time about trying for that twenty. I mean, it wasn't like he was hesitating because he didn't feel confident, but it was like he was taking his time so everybody could get a real good look at him. And there wasn't an eye in the whole place that wasn't looking at him that I could tell. Even the older ladies who were in the little room making the hot dogs and Frito pies and selling coffee stopped what they were doin' to peer over the counter and look at Anderson. And the lady who was watching the door and taking the admission money and stamping hands and the two tribal policemen who were watching out to be sure there wasn't no monkey-business outside—they all came to the door of the gym to watch Anderson George make a try for that money.

And he danced in a smaller and smaller circle round and round till he was right there looking down at where that twenty-dollar bill was lying on the floor with its one corner folded up to where, if you could ever reach down that low with your teeth, you could grab ahold of the money. I would have thought that Anderson would do the splits since that's how the guys who got the closest to the money had done it. But maybe he had learned from watching the others that that really wasn't the best way to try. Anyhow, what Anderson did was to put his left foot right there beside the twenty and slowly, with the beat of the Salt River Drum, start to stretch his right leg straight out behind him, bending his left knee and holding his arms out to the sides like an airplane for balance. And you could see that his eyes were gazing at that money and his concentration was strong and sure.

I don't think Bernadette was even breathing by that time. I know I wasn't because even though I wanted Anderson to get that money, I didn't think he could do it without falling down. And I must have reached over and took ahold of my sister's arm and hung on tight—so tight that it made red and purple welts on her arm that she showed me later on in the pickup. But she was just sitting there like she was glued to those bleachers, with her hands still up to her cheeks, her eyes wide and glistening in those bright gym lights.

And Anderson was bending lower and lower until it looked like he couldn't go no lower and you could tell from clear up where we were sitting how his teeth were clenched and his whole body seemed to be quivering from straining and trying so hard and the veins on his neck were stickin' out like ropes. And then his teeth were just a couple of inches from the money but everybody could see that he wouldn't be able to bend his neck any farther down and it looked like he was gonna have to get disqualified.

Then, all of a sudden, Anderson just sort of dove at that twenty-dollar bill! Grabbing it in his teeth and at the same time turning over in mid-air so that even though he landed on his back, his knees and his hands never even touched the floor and you could see that he had that money in his teeth!

Oh man, you should have heard the commotion then! All the other drums picked right up and played along with the Salt River guys and the other dancers just about all broke into a war dance and the people clapped and cheered. And Anderson George, well, he jumped to his feet with that twenty-dollar bill still in his teeth and danced around and around that gym floor—cockier than *ever!*

I was still grabbing onto Bernadette's arm and shaking her and laughing and I remember how I looked at her and went to hug her and noticed that she still had her hands to her face and there were these great big tears rolling down her face but she was smiling and grinning and nodding her head 'cause lots of the people sitting around us were raising a ruckus, hollering stuff at her like *"All Right, Bernadette!"* and *"Hey, Lefthand! Did you see that?"* and congratulating her like *she'd* been the one dancing and slapping her on the back and all. Oh, it was something, all right.

And Tom George—I remember real clear how I looked over and saw him sitting there beating his drum with the others and how his face was real straight and calm-looking like nothing unusual had even happened. But I know to this day that really his heart was about to explode inside his chest because he was so proud of his brother. To tell you the truth, I think everybody in that place was proud of Anderson George that night.

And after that one dance was finally finished, everybody crowded up around Anderson, and Harrison Morning Gun was the first one up to shake his hand, which showed what a good sport he was I think. And Anderson George was just soaking it all up—all the attention and having all the young boys look up to him, and all. And then—and I think it was for the first time since that dance had started—I saw him glance up to where me and Bernadette was sitting and just a little flicker of a smile passed over his face and I can remember thinking how awful it would have been if he hadn't been successful.

Me and Bernadette talked about that dance all the way back to Dulce that night. She couldn't hardly wait to tell our Daddy all about it and her friends the next day. I mean, Bernadette had already won a whole lot of contests with her dancing—and in Oklahoma and in Colorado, too. But I don't remember seeing my sister any prouder and more excited than she was about that night and Anderson George.

▼▼▼

You know, Anderson wasn't drinking and actin' all strange too much back then.

I mean, at least it wasn't what you'd call a problem for him. Oh sure, sometimes he'd get pretty drunk in some bar where the oil field workers hung out—on Friday or Saturday night, mostly—and then maybe he'd have a bad hangover the next day. He wasn't what you picture when you think of a drunk person. He wasn't one to be a loud-mouth and start trouble. Even if I say he's a bastard now—and you would, too, if he killed your sister—I got to admit that he used to be okay. Like when he was dancing at that powwow down in Taos.

And Bernadette, she didn't drink at all. Daddy's brother, Bennie Lefthand, he was a real bad drinker and Bernadette always said she had had her fill of that kind of crap from seeing how awful it was for our Aunt Lupe and our cousins—never having anything nice and having an awful, old broken-down house where everybody avoided visiting because, like they said, that sorry drunk Bennie Lefthand lived there.

I guess I should say, though, that I have some powerful good memories of the times we went to visit with Aunt Lupe's family at Taos. I mean, it wasn't always so bad— Uncle Bennie's drinking, that is. Back then I guess we kids didn't even know he got drunk. It was like he could be on his good behavior when it was a special day and he knew that we were coming down from Dulce. I remember that we used to go and stay at their house at the Pueblo whenever there was some big doin's there.

Like on San Geronimo, which is their feast day down there. And Three Kings' Day in January when they get their new governor and war chief staffs and then have Buffalo Dances in the Plaza. The Buffalo Dance is held in the afternoon and I remember how there would always be a lot of tourists there standing around gawking and showing off their fancy fur coats and trying to look like Indians and all. You know, Tom George always had this joke about how one of the biggest tribes nowadays—about the only tribe that keeps on growin' by leaps and bounds—is made up of the *Wannabes*. That's what Tom called all the white people who wanna be Indians.

Anyway, talking about Wannabes and their fancy fur coats makes me think about one time on Christmas Eve when they have the big bonfires at the Pueblo, and on this particular Christmas Eve it was real cold and the wind was blowing pretty good and there was a bunch of us standing by this one big piñon fire and somebody—I think it was Bernadette—said that something smelled awful funny like it was hair burning. And then when we started lookin' around to see where that smell was coming from we noticed there was this white guy standing there in this full-length fur coat that looked like it was made out of coyote skins. If it was coyote skins then it was pretty dumb on his part to wear them at Indian doin's since Indians aren't all that fond of coyotes in the first place—and especially Navajos, who have a real thing about coyotes. Anyway, it could've been a rabbit skin coat for all I know, but it was sure enough fancy, and the guy had on a big cowboy hat with an expensive-looking silver concho hatband and he'd turned his back to the fire so as to warm his butt, I guess. And we could see that his fancy fur coat was smoking and curling up to beat the band from where the heat from that pitchy piñon wood fire was singeing it. Man, I bet that coat cost that guy a whole bunch of money, whatever it was made of. He was very foolish to wear it there that night is all I got to say about it.

I remember those big bonfires were always real smoky and hot. Every year our clothes would smell smoky for the longest time after we'd been at Taos on Christmas

Eve . . . and our faces would look smudgy from all the black soot on them. One time Bernadette even complained that standing around those fires turned her hair black. Of course that was very funny since there wasn't any way my sister's hair could have gotten any blacker than it already was.

One of my most favorite times was every year on the night of Three Kings' Day when the Taos families and their visitors would gather in their houses around a warm fire or wood stove and push the furniture back up against the wall and tell stories and visit and catch up on the news while they waited for the different dancers and singers to come by the house and come inside and sing and dance. Uncle Bennie would sometimes doze off in his chair and we kids would giggle because we thought he was funny— but I guess it wasn't funny to Aunt Lupe and the older people who knew why he was dozing off.

Sometimes there'd be maybe eight or ten different groups that would be going around—some of them were kiva boys and some were just dancers. Any house where they saw that the lights were burning and the door was open, well, they'd come right in and dance and some of the younger teenagers who were out following them around would stand at the door and watch. Then when they were finished dancing, whoever was the head woman in that house—my Aunt Lupe in our case—would give this one guy who was carrying around a big sack for the dancers and singers a bunch of fruit and maybe a loaf of bread that she'd baked that morning. And if one of the dancers was real good or extra fancy or it looked like they'd gone to a lot of trouble to prepare for the evening or it was particularly cold outside or whatever, somebody, like maybe one of the men or women visitors, would stand up and go right over and put some money into that dancer's hand—usually it was a dollar.

Every once in awhile some of the dancers would be made up pretty wild and it would scare the children. Usually, though, it was a fun kinda scared, not like when we were little and would go down there to San Geronimo and those Black Eyes came around all painted up black and white with corn husks stuck in their hair and chased all the children and threw some of them in the river and anyway scared us real bad. Oh Lord, I remember one year especially that this big fat one scared me so bad I wet my pants—really, I did. I was so scared and embarrassed that I had bad dreams for a long time, but I can tell you that for a whole year whenever my Daddy told me to behave all he had to do was mention that he'd get the Black Eyes to come and take care of me and I would straighten up and fly right, believe you me.

Those were some good times we had back then. But it seems like when you grow older the troubles start coming more often.

▼▼▼

It was surprising to me about Tom George, surprising that he wasn't a drinker, that is.

I don't know why that was, since in most things Anderson and Tom George were like peas in a pod. But of course Tom'd always go along with Anderson to the bars and stuff, even though Tom never drank whiskey or beer or wine—least ways not that I ever heard about. Just orange pop or coffee. I think maybe he figured he needed to have a clear head to drive that new pickup truck of theirs. And it's a good thing, too, because there's always a lot of drunk drivers out on the highways you know—especially around a border town on weekends. Daddy always said, you want to take your life in your hands, just try driving on a Saturday night around Gallup or on that twenty-five mile stretch of two-lane between there and Window Rock.

I guess the bosses at the oil fields up at Farmington were usually real good to Anderson and Tom George when it came to getting a little extra time off to go to rodeos and powwows that first summer. I think they were both pretty good workers and didn't take advantage of the bosses' good nature like some of the other guys did. Plus, it was hard not to like those two—always joking and smiling and not mouthing off or complaining. So almost every weekend that first summer after high school there was big doin's somewhere—a rodeo or powwow of some kind—and those guys were always on the go. And if it was at all possible, Bernadette was there too. The boys would drive over here to Dulce and pick her up, either that or else she'd get one of her girlfriends to go and Daddy would let her take the Ford. I think that Bernadette was really always Daddy's favorite—I know it almost killed him when she died. I guess you could say I was even a little bit jealous of her back then, her being the main attraction all the time—everybody always talking about Bernadette this and Bernadette that. It's just that now I miss her so bad—I'd be glad to have her be the center of attention.

I only wish me and Daddy could at least talk about her sometimes, but we don't. Like we never were allowed to talk about our mother after she went off to the Indian Hospital over in Albuquerque when I was eight—for some tests, they said—and then she just never came back home. Even though I was just a little girl when she went away, I can still remember the times when she would hold me on her lap and tell me that I was her special girl—it made me feel like I was . . . I dunno, like I was worthwhile. We never did talk about her after she was gone, though. You know, it's some Indians' way not to talk about someone who's died.

The first premise of the Navaho Way is that life is very, very dangerous.

—Clyde Kluckhohn
and Dorothea Leighton
The Navaho (1946)

Starr

Winter came early the year Bernadette died.

It seemed like there wasn't really even an autumn at all that year. And autumn was as pretty a season as there was up in that Dulce country. The winters were miserable—cold and gray for the most part. And if there was one thing worse than winter there, it had to be the spring—when all the ice and snow melted and that cold and gray and miserable little town was bogged down in a sea of brown mud.

God, how I hated that place in the springtime.

So I spent the entire November that year lost in some book or else watching the television shows that somehow got beamed down into the big ugly satellite dish Rounder paid some men to install right outside the living room window to block the only decent view I had of the mountains. Reading and watching television shows and drinking booze to keep from going out of my fucking mind.

You know, all those television shows that during November seem to be nothing but the traditional Peanuts and Snoopy Thanksgiving crap and Assassination Anniversary Specials. If you don't want to look at cartoon characters dressed like pilgrims, your only other choice is to watch the endless reruns in slow motion of somebody's jerky home movie of JFK's brains being splattered all over Jackie's pretty pink dress and then her frantically crawling out across the trunk of that big, fancy black limousine—like who the hell wouldn't try and save their ass in a spot like that? And as if that isn't enough, then we get to see that black and white replay of that gun-slinging strip joint owner Jack Ruby blowing away that little pinko punk Oswald in a Dallas police station basement on national TV.

Jesus!

Mostly I read at night. Sometimes, when I couldn't get to sleep, I'd read all night—right up until morning. My days consisted mainly of watching television and checking the mail at the post office—there wasn't any mail delivery in Dulce. I was looking for letters from old friends back in the city—New York City—who could tell me about what was going on back where people were still alive, where they still had parties and fine restaurants and delis and department stores and taxis and other evidence of civilization. And so that I might at least get the announcements that most of the art galleries and museums in Santa Fe and Taos and even Scottsdale would send whenever there was to be an opening or a special show. And then I'd get in that big-assed Suburban and drive to wherever the opening happened to be—anyplace was better than Dulce, New Mexico.

Hey, those gallery owners were smart to send me announcements of their openings. I mean, I was a damned good customer. They knew I'd buy whatever new work of art they had to offer. Mostly I'd buy the work just to show those suckers that I *could* buy it. But I also bought it so I could surround myself with fine and pretty things in that godforsaken place I lived. The rest of Dulce's population may have considered those god-awful paintings of Jesus or Elvis or big semi-trucks on black velvet to be the highest form of art, but I sure as hell didn't.

◆

If I were to tell the truth—and usually I get myself in trouble because I do tell the truth—I married Rounder because I thought it would be fun being married to somebody famous. And to be perfectly honest I have to say that Rounder Stubbs married me because he liked the idea that I was a tall blond model from New York.

Being a popular singer and songwriter, Rounder was fairly well-off in the money department—even rich you might say. He had come to New York from Nashville and I first met him at a cocktail party given by this faggotty little fashion designer that I knew who everybody's heard of. I remember at the time thinking it was cute the way Rounder blushed when Peter introduced him at the party.

"Listen up everybody," Peter had lisped. "I want you all to meet Mr. Jim Bob Rounder Stubbs. Mr. Jim Bob here is a fairly famous hillbilly cowboy singing star who spent all day today driving around Manhattan in his great big gorgeous powder blue Greyhound bus with his name painted in gold letters on the side! Don't you just love it? I know I do!

"God, what great big balls this handsome young cowboy must have to do something like that! At least I guess he does—I confess I haven't gotten to check that out . . . yet!"

And I remember how I was struck by Rounder's genuine shyness and the fact that he was actually awed by the kind of people that showed up at Peter's parties. That and the whole idea that he was in New York City.

Later on, when we left the party together, Peter swished over to say good-bye at the door.

"Now you be careful, cowboy," he winked at Rounder and pursed his lips in an obscene kiss. "These big city girls can and will fuck your eyes out before you can say 'Aw shucks, ma'am.'"

And of course he was right.

◆

Rounder and I lived together for nearly a year before we finally got married and moved to New Mexico. Talk about the fast lane—that year was a blur in more ways than one. We lived *between* my flat in New York and Rounder's condo in Nashville—mostly on that powder blue tour bus with the guys in Rounder's band. God, it was all just one big party on the road. During that one year I saw the insides of more civic center auditoriums and dance hall honkey tonks than I care to recall. Mostly we traveled in the West and Southwest—California, Texas, Oklahoma . . . places like that. But back in those days Rounder was popular all over, and so we went wherever he'd been booked to play. Lots of times I didn't know where we were—and neither did Rounder.

Those were crazy times. I know this—I may have been drinking quite a bit in those days, but nothing like Rounder. He drank more than anyone I've ever known. And he drank straight whiskey. The thing was, Rounder could drink enough to put a normal man away for good, but he never seemed to get drunk. Why, I've seen him play concerts and do live television interviews when he'd been drinking for three days straight without a break of any kind. Most people couldn't have stood up as loaded as Rounder was, much less sung songs and made sense. And on top of that, all of us used marijuana—Mexican "boo smoke" Rounder called it—and of course we were heavy into cocaine. The thing is, there was enough money for whatever we wanted, and believe me, we wanted it all.

Then I got scared.

We were in Houston, where Rounder and the band were appearing as the headline entertainers for some big rodeo. As usual, after the show we partied the rest of the night away. When I finally woke up late the next afternoon I realized that I was feeling about as good as I was likely going to feel all day—and believe me, I felt like shit. I was hung over from the booze, the grass and the blow— not to mention the lack of anything approaching normal sleep. Then I looked in the mirror and felt even worse. I've always been fair-complexioned, and to look into a mirror and see black pouches under my eyes and tiny purple and red veins standing out on my skin . . . well, it was more than I could take. I told Rounder right then and there that I couldn't keep it up any longer.

"Something's got to change," I told him. "Look at me, goddammit—I look like an old woman!"

"Ah, baby, you look great," Rounder lied.

"Great, my ass," I yelled at him. "I look like hell and you know it—and I feel worse than I look. I'm serious Rounder, either we slow down . . . settle down somewhere and start living halfway normal lives, or I'm outta here. I mean it, I'm going back to the city!"

I asked for it. And I got it. Because that very summer we got married and built a real house. Not in New York like I'd expected—but on the edge of a goddamned Indian reservation in northern New Mexico!

Rounder had been there a couple of times before we'd met. Apparently he went because they shoot deer or bears or something in the woods up there and so he had a real liking for the place for some reason. I guess something about shooting big guns at little animals must have made him feel more like a man and so he associated Dulce with his manliness. Anyway, Rounder said he'd always wanted to live in New Mexico and that Dulce was a real beautiful place.

I'll admit it wasn't hard for him to convince me. I was scared and just wanted to slow down awhile. I felt then like anything was better than living on a goddamned bus.

And for the first year or so things *were* okay. I kept busy decorating the house and collecting cowboy and

Indian art. I really got into the whole Southwest artsy-fartsy thing, too. I even dressed the part—wore silver and turquoise jewelry and leather jackets with beadwork and cowboy boots that I had made especially to order by some guy in El Paso. And I taught myself to ride horses and got Rounder to hire some local Indians to build a barn and corral and some pens down below the house where we could keep the paint horses I bought to raise.

And would you believe it? I actually got to be a real homebody. I guess you could say I got completely caught up in my own little world and in my books. I got to where I wanted to know everything there was to know about the Indian people and the way they lived, and the only way to do that was to read about them. Lord knows you couldn't get them to tell you anything about themselves. My house was comfortable and except when it was somewhere I really wanted to see, I stopped going on the road with Rounder and the band. To tell the truth, I don't think he cared much one way or the other. Whatever else he was, Rounder was a real professional when it came to his music and it was hard for him to work up much interest in anything else when he had a gig. And at least when he was on tour he didn't have to listen to me bitching about him doing liquor and drugs. During that first year in New Mexico I stopped doing dope altogether and cut way back on the booze—a little sherry in the afternoons and a bottle of good wine with dinner was the extent of my mood elevators for awhile there. Of course Rounder didn't change a bit in that respect. And since he was away so much of the time, I didn't really nag him about it when he was home.

I can tell you that my husband got the name "Rounder" in the first place on account of he's always been so crazy. I don't mean that he's unbalanced in the way that a lot of folks are . . . I just mean he's a crazy man

. . . in that kind of a wild and rowdy sort of way.

It's certainly no secret that he likes to drink. And that he likes to drink a lot. Mind you, I've never seen him pass out, or throw up, or in any way indicate that he's lost control because of his heavy drinking. But on the other hand, what I have seen him do is bizarre . . . I mean a *lot* bizarre.

Like once when I wasn't home he put a lawn sprinkler in the middle of the living room and turned it on full blast and then drove off. All because I'd jumped on him for tracking mud in the house. Then for a long time afterward he'd look very hurt and sheepish any time he'd catch me looking at something that had been ruined in that episode—like the big water stain on that expensive Navajo rug that hangs over the fireplace.

Whenever somebody came to visit us he'd even make a point of showing them where the wood flooring was warped. "Isn't that pitiful?" he'd say, pointing to the damage and shaking his head sadly. "Now there's a fine example of my handiwork."

But even feeling sorry for some of his pranks didn't seem to cure him. Like sometimes he would get all the guys in the band to line up with him along one side of the bus and drop their pants and press their bare cheeks up against the windows as they drove through some small, backwater town.

"Ah, hell, Starr," he'd say when I complained. "These aren't your New Yorkers . . . these are just plain folks who ain't never had a chance to see anything like that before. This is just real special to them—seein' a famous person moon 'em—don't you know they'll always remember this as one of the highlights of their life and end up buyin' more records, too?"

The scary thing was, I think maybe he was right.

And he had somehow got hold of one of those red lights like unmarked police cars and volunteer firemen use that plug into cigarette lighters and that they then stick up on top of their cars when they're on their way to the scene of a crime or a fire. Rounder used to like to get up on some overpass out on the interstate highway and wait until a family of vacationers in a station wagon came along and then he'd zoom down behind them honking and with that red light flashing and wave them over and then lecture them on how they were speeding on American Indian land and give them autographed record albums when they recognized who he was.

Then there was the time when we were riding an elevator in a Hyatt Regency hotel in Fort Worth and it was full of these little old women who'd been attending some kind of convention or craft show or something. Rounder grinned at them all real big and tipped his hat as he announced that he hoped weren't none of them particularly light sleepers.

"I'm headin' upstairs to have big sex with this tall white woman here," he said. "And I 'spect the noise of her happy hollerin' is likely to get powerful loud."

Then he bowed real low when we got off on our floor.

Gracie

I don't think I mentioned that our mother was of the Jicarilla Apache Tribe, which is the reason why we happen to live in Dulce.

Daddy's mostly Pueblo—his people are from Taos—but he says that he's part Mexican, too, even though I think he's kind of ashamed of that part of him. Anyway, I figure that's why Bernadette didn't mind that Anderson George was a Navajo from over by Chinle. Our Daddy had pretty much convinced us that the worst thing for an Indian girl to do would be to marry a white boy or even a *black* white boy. He always was sayin' that if your own tribe is too small to find somebody to marry that you're not related to, then it's okay to look somewhere else. As long as you stick to Indians so as not to bring shame on your family, that is. Of course, he always used to say that before Bernadette chose Anderson—see, I don't think he ever thought about Navajos when he was talkin' that way, what with Pueblo people not being real fond of Navajos in the first place they wouldn't come to his mind I don't think. He used to joke that all the single girls at Taos were either his cousins or else they weighed three hundred pounds and that the first time he saw our mother dance at a gathering down there, he decided right then and there that he'd even go live with those Apaches if that's what it took to get her.

Daddy says our mother was a very good dancer back then and that that's probably where Bernadette got her ability. He told us that our mother was the most gentle and graceful traditional dancer he'd ever seen and that her feet were especially small and dainty and that he never could understand how she ended up with a name like Iron Moccasin in the first place. He said that was kind of like a white person being called "Lead Foot" on account of them being so clumsy. He was always shaking his head and remarking on how even though he always favored his right hand he still ended up being named Lefthand. It was his idea that what he called our "whitemen names" didn't mean a whole lot to Indian people mainly on account of the fact Indians mostly got those names stuck on to them when the whites couldn't pronounce their real names anyhow.

Of course Iron Moccasin was just our mother's name before she married our father—her whole name back then was Mary Theresa Lourdes Iron Moccasin, which goes to show that she was pretty strong in the Catholic religion, or at least our grandmother must have been since she gave her those religious names in the first place. I say religious names because I figure everybody knows that Mary and Theresa are names right out of the Bible. What some people might not know is that Lourdes is the name of the place where a miracle is supposed to have happened a long time ago, over in France I think, or maybe it was England . . . I always get those foreign places confused. Anyway, they say that this particular miracle took place when a girl named Bernadette had a vision of the Virgin Mary and even got to talk to her. Later on they made the girl into a saint on account of what all had happened. And I guess you know how every day of the year has its own saint? Well, the saint for the day my sister was born—which was April 16th—turned out to be Saint Bernadette, and our mother took that to be a special sign instead of just a co-incidence and so named her in honor of Saint Bernadette.

In case you're wondering, I don't really know how come I happened to be named Grace. I doubt that it was because I was graceful since I'm not particularly. Maybe it was because my mother was so full of grace.

▼▼▼

Dee's Place is where my Daddy always spends quite a bit of his time whenever he's not working.

I know you're probably thinking that anybody who hangs around a place like Dee's where they sell beer and wine—that they're probably a good-for-nothing. But Dee's is not one of them nasty bars where the whole place smells like stale beer and vomit all the time. I been in some of those places over by Farmington where it always makes you think that someone has just taken a leak on a hot stove, and that's just in the bar. The bathrooms in some of those places are so filthy that some of the regulars go out to the parking lots whenever they have to take a pee—even the women. But that's not the way it is over at Dee's.

My Daddy's friend Benjamin, he's the cook there. The way it works is, they can serve you beer and wine only if you get some food, too. The place is called Dee's because Benjamin's wife is named Dee. Actually, it used to be called Bill & Dee's and was owned by Dee and her ex-husband, Bill. They weren't neither one of them Indian people. They came to Dulce from up at Durango, Colorado, where Bill had a welding shop up until the time he fell off a truckload of oilfield pipe and broke his back and went on disability. Then him and Dee moved down here and took over this place.

They say back then Benjamin Begay was just a regular at the place, like some of the other men in town. Benjamin's a Navajo who was one of the code talkers back in World War II—Daddy says that was when the government went out on the reservation and rounded up a bunch of Indians to be in the Marines so they could talk on the radios in Navajo and the Japs wouldn't understand what all was goin' on. Benjamin tells some real funny stories about how him and his buddies used to bullshit the Marine officers a lot without them knowing it by really just shootin' the breeze on those radios about half the time. Of course, he won't put up with nobody *else* making fun, though. He says that America couldn't never have won that war if it hadn't been for the fact of the code talkers confusing them Japs.

Anyway, they say Dee sort of took a shine to Benjamin hanging around all the time, and it got to where he was helping out around the place sometimes—washing dishes or sweeping up. Of course, that's not *all* he was doing as it turns out, because after a few months of Benjamin helping out, Bill just up and took off for California one night—or Dee ran him off, depending on who's telling the story—and quick as you please, Benjamin Begay ups and moves his stuff into the house with Dee. They say that was in 1975, and that it wasn't until sometime in 1979 that Dee one day got some divorce papers in the mail from Bill and pretty soon after that her and Benjamin got married. It's funny, but there just ain't a whole lot of places that sell beer and wine that I know of have Indians working in them, but somehow or other Dee got Benjamin to stop drinking altogether and even got him to start attending AA meetings a couple of times a week—for awhile anyway—so it works out pretty good.

Sometimes people tease old Benjamin and call it Benjamin's Place, but if Dee's around and hears them, she'll go to ranting and raving so bad and hollering that this is by-god *her* place and they better not any of them forget it least of all not Benjamin, and people have to be pretty careful what they say. Usually though, Dee's lying around in her bathrobe over at the house or if she is at the place it's just on account of the TV there gets better reception than the one at the house.

They have a jukebox that plays mostly just country singers. People like Willie Nelson and George Jones. But the one song that gets played more than anything else—whenever somebody has a quarter or else when Benjamin puts in money on the house, that is—is that guy by the name of Johnny Paycheck singing "Take This Job and Shove It." And every time somebody plays that song all the guys in the place—especially those that have jobs with the BIA—go to acting all big-shot like maybe they're gonna tell off their boss over there or something. Of course they never do when the next day comes, 'cause they know they'd just get fired and they're apt to lose their jobs fast enough as it is just by drinkin' too much on a weeknight and not showing up for work the next morning on account of they have a bad hangover. So I figure either way, that Paycheck guy is a bad influence on the ones who have jobs. I mean, even if they don't have the nerve to go tell their boss to shove it, whenever they listen to that song they just drink more and act cockier and maybe not get up when their wife or the alarm clock tells 'em to the next morning. It ends up the same, either way.

On this one particular night I remember it was just Benjamin and Daddy and me and George Otero who were in the place. In case you're wonderin' why I was there, well, ever since our mother died Benjamin and Dee sort of took special care of Bernadette and me—you know, looked out to make sure we had dinner if Daddy was working late and everything. Anyway, I spent a lot of time over there, especially after Bernadette went away to school and I was so lonesome.

George Otero always used to sit by himself at this one

table over by the men's room, which if you ask me, proved that guy was really just a crazy half-Mexican, half-Apache since the smell alone over there from the disinfectant that Dee insists on Benjamin mopping the floor with would just about gag a maggot. And matter of fact, George always was about three-quarters crazy even when he hadn't been drinking—which wasn't very often by the way—so it's just as well that he liked to sit there by himself and nurse a grilled-cheese sandwich and let Benjamin or me bring him a fresh beer every once in awhile.

Anyway, pretty soon in walks a couple of white guys who apparently didn't find the soap smell all that offensive but still sat up at the counter, ordered cheeseburgers and a couple of long-neck Buds, and announced big as you please that they were staying over in Chama at one of those lodges that caters to elk hunters and had wandered up to Dulce looking for, they said, some local Indian color. I tell you, they were a right funny looking pair, those two. The one was fat and red-faced and was dressed up like some duck hunter in one of those sports magazines—you know, with canvas pants tucked into the top of his boots, a red plaid flannel shirt, and a camouflage jacket. The guy with him was tall and skinny, in bluejeans and denim shirt and wearing a shooting vest and a day-glow, orange-billed cap.

Benjamin was sitting on his regular tall stool behind the counter, which in Dee's is shaped like an "L," and Daddy was at his normal place on the short leg of the "L." I was in the kitchen where I could see and hear what all was going on. These two hunters, they sat down at the other side of the counter so that it was like the four of them—the hunters and Daddy and Benjamin—were at a table. George Otero just sat at his seat glaring at the top of the table where some sorry people have carved their initials and probably some dirty words that Dee hasn't discovered yet and made Benjamin rub off with sandpaper. Anyway, George wasn't in on the conversation at all.

"Whoo-boy," the fat man in the red plaid shirt says. "This is some dead town you got here."

His friend, the tall, skinny guy with a burr haircut under his day-glow cap, had a pair of ears that stuck out from his head so abruptly they looked to have been drawn on as some kind of joke by one of those guys at the state fair over in Albuquerque that draw the funny cartoons of regular people for five dollars. Anyway, this skinny man laughed at everything the fat man said even when it wasn't supposed to be funny.

"Hey, Chief!" The fat man was talking to Daddy. "What's your tribe do around here after the sun goes down? Besides hide all the women, that is."

The skinny guy laughed appreciatively like he thought the fat man had made a real funny joke.

"Naw, seriously now, Chief, you all can't tell me that this is all there is to Dulce, New Mexico. Goddammit fellers, we're from Lubbock, Texas, and we're used to the high life." And then the man grins real big.

"I never been to Lubbock," Daddy said.

"No shit? You ever hear of Buddy goddamn Holly, Chief? Ugly little fucker, but the sumbitch was one hell of a rock and roll star back in the '50s. Hey, I understand Rounder Stubbs lives around these parts, that right?"

Daddy didn't answer, but the man went on like he had.

"Can't really understand why, can you, Bubba?"

The other man grinned and shook his head dumbly.

"Why, they even got a life-sized statue of Buddy down at the Civic Center in Lubbock—white people *and* niggers come from all over just to pay their respects to his memory. Shit fire, if old Buddy hadn't gone and got his ass killed in that plane crash back east, people all over the world would be callin' *him* the King instead of that peckerwood Elvis Presley, ain't that a fact, Bubba?"

The skinny man grinned from enormous ear to enormous ear. "Yup, that sure as hell is a fact, Hoss," he says. "'Peggy Sue' was always 'bout my favorite song that old Buddy Holly did."

"Aw, *bullshit*," the fat man roared. "'Peggy Sue' is goddamned amateurish compared to 'Not Fade Away,' wouldn't you agree, Chief?"

"My name is Lefthand." Daddy spoke without looking directly at the man. "Edwin Lefthand. And I'd appreciate it if you don't call me 'Chief.'"

"Aw shit-fire, old buddy . . . I didn't mean nothin' derogatory by it. Back home in Lubbock I got several good friends are full-blood Indians. Hell, I even let 'em come to my house and have dinner with me and the wife and kids sometimes, and they all know that 'Chief' ain't nothin' but a term of endearment to me. Why, if the truth be known, I'm part Indian myownself—Cherokee tribe, out of Oklahoma—and damn sure enough proud of it. Can't get much more American than that—Trail of Tears an' ever'thing. Goddamned Cherokees are a right progressive tribe, too—I mean, damn if they ain't got a woman for their chief . . . gal by the name of *Mankiller*. Now how you figure a woman to end up with a name like that?"

Bubba grinned real big. "Hell, maybe she killed her a man one time, Hoss."

The red-faced man ignored his friend. He took a big bite of his sandwich and a swig of beer and then looked at my Daddy. "Hey, and speakin' of names, what the hell kinda name is 'Lefthand,' anyway?"

He said the name again. "*Lefthand* . . . I mean, is that your honest-to-god Christian name or is it just the American translation of some Indian word?"

I had the feeling that those two were not really ornery,

just stupid like so many of their kind tend to be. They weren't actually meaning to be insulting—they just were. It was their nature and I could tell that Daddy and Benjamin figured to just ignore it as best they could.

Benjamin could see me at the kitchen door where I stood listening. I saw him wink at me. "Say, Eddie," he says. "Just how *do* we Indians get our names?"

Daddy picked up on the joke and fell right in step. I mean, it wasn't the first time they'd pulled this one. In fact, I'm almost ashamed to tell it now since it's such an old joke and I figure everybody knows how it comes out already. But anyhow, my Daddy picked up on it.

"You mean you don't really know, Benjamin?" he asked.

"Naw," says Benjamin. "I just figured we got our names from the Great White Father in Washington after he couldn't spell our Indian names when it came time to send us our tax bills."

"Oh, hell no, Benjamin," Daddy said. "It's a long-standing tradition among all Indian tribes that as soon as a new baby arrives in the teepee, the brave who is that child's father throws open the flap to the teepee and walks outside into the great outdoors where the Great Spirit is waiting to reveal to the brave warrior just what that newborn papoose is to be named."

As he's talking, Daddy's stood up and is making sweeping motions with his arms and gesturing with his hands like the old stereotyped noble savage making sign language in John Wayne movies. I glance over at Benjamin, who winks at me again. The two white hunters are listening intently.

"The Great Spirit then reveals the name He has chosen according to what it is that the father first sees upon stepping out of the teepee. For example, when my sister was born, the first thing my father saw when he looked out of our teepee door was a young deer jumping over a fallen log. So my sister's name is *Graceful Deer Leaping*."

All this time the two white men are listening and nodding their heads—certain that they're hearing real important Indian lore that most white men can only guess at.

"Why, your own wife," Daddy glances toward Benjamin. "Although her white name is *Dee*, as you know her Indian name is *Lovely Morning Star*, which is what her father first saw immediately after she was born."

Benjamin looks with deep seriousness at the two Texans. "You know gentlemen," he said, "Mr. Lefthand here is a very famous Apache Medicine Man. You're just real lucky that you got to even hear that story."

The fat man nods his head gravely. "Yes indeed, and we are honored, Chief Lefthand. And we'd like to buy you a cold beer for sharing with us the story of how it is that you real Indians come to have such wonderful names."

"Why, thank you very much," my father says, as Benjamin sets another can of beer down beside the one he's drinking.

Then Daddy sort of leans toward the two and lowers his voice. "But you know, this Great Spirit thing doesn't always work out so well."

"It don't?" says Bubba.

"What do you mean by that?" says the fat man.

"Well now, you take that big fellow sitting there all by himself over by the men's room," Daddy nods slightly toward where George Otero sits scowling. "That man sitting over there is named *Ah-hi-di-dail Lha-cha-eh*."

The one called Bubba nods his head and stares at George like he understands he's hearing another wonderful secret.

The red-faced man looks back at Daddy. "So?" he says.

"Well, *Ah-hi-di-dail Lha-cha-eh* in English means *Two Dogs Fucking*." The two men look intently toward where

George is. The one named Bubba, his lower jaw is slack and his mouth hangs partly open. Then this kind of funny look starts to pass over the fat man's face—like he's beginnin' to figure out that he's being made fun of.

And just then Benjamin says in this real confidential tone of voice, "But you know, you probably ought not to call him that to his face."

"Aw, shit!" the fat man says and stands up real fast. He takes a ten-dollar bill out of his billfold and throws it down on the counter.

"Bubba, these assholes ain't doin' nothin' but pissin' on our shoes! Now eat your goddamned burger and let's get the hell out of this stinkin' place."

As they were leaving, the skinny guy, Bubba, stopped by where George was sitting and said, "Just what *is* your name, buddy?" And George just looked up at him and grinned real big to show how he was missing some of his teeth in front and that Bubba guy, why he high-tailed it right on out the door.

Yes sir, we all got a real big laugh out of that one. From the way he kept on grinning, I'd say that George Otero enjoyed the joke too, even though I don't think he was able to hear the whole conversation and I know he didn't hear what my Daddy said his name was . . . or at least I hope he didn't.

Like I said, that was just a joke . . . a really old joke.

Most of us do have Indian names, though—those ones of us that have been raised traditional, anyway. Of course it's not a good idea to tell people what your Indian name is—they say that it's the only way you can be witched by an evil person—if he knows your personal name. That by just saying your name a certain way in one of his chants a witch can cause you to get sick and even die. But I'll tell you what that Anderson George's personal Indian name is—it's *Pretty Soldier*, is what it is. I don't really care much one way or the other if he gets bad luck or even witched, for one thing—in fact I hope he does. And for another thing, I always thought that *Pretty Soldier* was just a real neat name. Of course I won't tell what mine is, but believe me, it ain't nearly as neat as *Pretty Soldier*. Or as *Morning Rain*, which was Bernadette's.

▼▼▼

There really isn't what you'd call a main street in Dulce, New Mexico. There's the area just off the highway where there's the bank and the grocery store and the tribal offices and all, but it's not like most towns.

The big new motel is the only attraction for people going down the highway. Except I guess it's not really what you'd call a "motel" since they gave it the name Big Valley Inn. There's another motel in town, but it's really just made out of what looks like these little old-timey trailer houses parked in a row and anyway is real tiny and they don't get any business to speak of now that the big new one's open. Especially since most of the business except for elk hunters is BIA workers who come to check on things—or should I say when they come to Boss Indians Around, since that's what we say BIA stands for. And anyway then those guys stay at the new place since they ain't payin' the bill anyhow and so don't mind that it costs twice as much.

The new place is really kind of fancy for a town the size of Dulce. It's got a pretty good restaurant and a gift shop that sells some of the baskets and beadwork and other crafts that's done around here and they even have a room where you can rent video movies if you got one of those machines at your house to watch it on. And I guess a lot of folks do, because there's always a bunch of old ladies and kids in there renting movies. And they hold the bingo games in a big meeting room there on Friday nights and Saturday afternoons. Lots of white people come to play bingo since the only place you can legally gamble for money in New Mexico is on Indian land. And since the place is really owned by the Jicarilla Tribe, some of the Indians around here have even got jobs there. In fact, before she got the job working for that singer and his wife outside of town, Bernadette worked at the new motel that first summer after she came back from school over in Santa Fe. She was a waitress in the restaurant mostly but sometimes she was working up in the gift shop. I worked for awhile there too, as a maid, but after Bernadette got killed I had to quit so I could stay to home and take care of the baby.

I said that there's a grocery store across from the new motel. Actually, it's called a shopping center even though it's just one store—not like the shopping centers I've seen in Albuquerque and even Santa Fe. Still, it has lots of stuff like tools and saddles and shirts and shoes . . . not just groceries. You can get just about whatever you need in that place. Like the fancy Pendleton wool blankets that Indians have liked to wear around for about as long as anybody can remember. And by the way they sell them blankets for sixty-five dollars in our store—and I'm talking about the exact same blankets that go for over a hundred in the white tourist towns. Of course, that's about the only example that I know of where you see Indians getting a better deal on something, though.

Except for Rounder Stubbs and his wife and a couple of BIA bigshots and the Indian Health Service nurse, all of which by the way are white, most everybody who lives around here is an Indian and real poor. One just naturally goes with the other, I guess.

The Stubbs don't actually live in Dulce, but out Highway 64 toward Lumberton about a mile and a half. They have a real big house that they built a few years back up on a little rise looking out across a pasture where they keep their good paint horses. I guess you could say their place is as close to a mansion as Dulce, New Mexico, is ever likely to see, even if it is made out of logs.

Rounder Stubbs is that country music singer from somewhere down in Texas who's been pretty successful I guess, and who's had a couple of his songs win some big awards that they give out to country singers. He may even have won some other awards, I don't really know. I've heard him sing on the radio and they have a couple of his songs on the jukebox in the bar at the new motel.

Anyhow, my sister had a job working at the Stubbs' house for awhile and I sometimes used to take and pick her up from there so that's how come I know about the house and some of the goings on in there. Later on, when she was fixin' to have her baby, Bernadette arranged it so that I went up and cleaned a couple of times a week. But back before that sometimes when I'd go to pick her up and nobody was home and Bernadette knew they wouldn't come driving up and surprise us like when they were together on one of those concert tours in their big fancy Greyhound bus that said "Rounder Stubbs and White Trash" in swirly gold letters on the side, Bernadette would tell me to come on in the house so that she could show me around. It was the biggest house I've ever been inside. There were four bedrooms and each one had its own bathroom and fireplace. The kitchen had two iceboxes and two stoves for cooking and beautiful copper pots and pans hanging on the walls and a huge rack that held more bottles of wine than most liquor stores probably have in them. And the living room, it was as big as our whole house and one wall in there was covered with autographed pictures of Rounder Stubbs smiling real big and standing beside other famous singers like Willie Nelson and Johnny Cash, and a whole lot of other people that I didn't recognize but who were probably real famous, too.

And guns. I don't know if Rounder Stubbs liked to go hunting or not, but I do know that he had a big thing about guns. I swear there was guns of all kinds everywhere. Some was hanging on the walls and some was in fancy cabinets with glass doors. There was guns leaning up in corners of rooms and Bernadette said there was guns in some of the drawers in the bedrooms and even in the bathroom that Rounder Stubbs used mostly.

And besides guns it seems like these people were into collecting Indian stuff, too—mostly Pueblo pottery and Plains beadwork. And Starr Stubbs, that's Rounder's wife's name, seemed to spend a lot of money on jewelry and art—paintings and statues mostly—done by Indian artists. And there was this one room in the house that looked to me almost like a library like you might see at school, with shelves that went all the way to the ceiling and a big desk and an easy chair where you could sit and read. And as near as I could tell just about every one of the books on those shelves were about Indians. There were history books and picture books and story books—some of them looked real old and some were brand new but there were books on just everything you'd want to know about all the different tribes there in that room. Bernadette said that it was Starr who was the reader in the family, that it was her who always seemed like she had her nose poked in a book and who had such an interest in Indian ways. I guess she used to question Bernadette about things that she'd read, you know, ask her if such and such was really true and all. Bernadette said that lots of times whatever it was Starr had read about was news to her—to Bernadette, that is—and that she'd learned a lot of interesting things she didn't know about our own people just by talking with Starr Stubbs about things she learned from those books.

Bernadette also said that Starr Stubbs used to be a big time clothes model back in New York City before she got married and that she keeps over a hundred pairs of high-heeled shoes in her bedroom closet—and that's not even counting all those pairs of cowboy boots that she's had handmade just for her since she moved out here. Some of those boots were really pretty silly looking if you ask me—I mean, they were in all colors like pink and light blue, and made out of all kinds of animal skins. Some of them even had feathers and silver and turquoise and diamonds on them. Course, I don't know if the diamonds were real or not, but they sure enough looked real. And the thing is, she would actually wear those boots whenever she went to pick up stuff at the store or when she went to the post office or the bank—even when it was muddy. And sometimes Starr Stubbs would go to the post office five or six times in one day, and wear different boots every time she went. At least that's what Benjamin Begay says, and he can see who comes and goes at the post office from over at the cafe.

Starr Stubbs has this real pretty long, curly blond hair. She's right proud of that hair, too, let me tell you. I figure she knows that light blond hair is just real unusual around here and she's one of those kinds who likes to stand out in a crowd if I ever saw one. Like the fact that she's not just pretty, but she's real tall for a woman—even for a white woman. It's funny, too, because her husband is pretty short and always wears these high-heeled cowboy boots and great big cowboy hats with extra tall crowns—just to make him look taller probably.

And it's funny how people react to her. Like whenever she's in the grocery store, pushing a cart around and going up and down the aisles, there's usually at least a couple of young girls following her around and looking up at that hair. And one time I remember seeing Starr

Stubbs eating lunch at the coffee shop over at the new motel and this little girl about four or five years old walked up to where she was sitting and just reached up and touched that yellow hair of hers. It was like she had never seen anything like that in her life before and wanted to know if it felt like regular hair. And I remember thinking at the time that Starr Stubbs was acting pretty nice about it because she didn't turn around or scold that little girl or anything.

But some of the older women in town, they don't think that Starr Stubbs is so nice to have around. You know how women can get real jealous when a prettier woman is in the neighborhood and the men keep noticing her—especially Indian women, and especially *Apache* Indian women. I've got to say that I never did trust Starr Stubbs all that much, and Bernadette even scolded me that I had a bad attitude when it came to Starr—that I wasn't acting any better than those women who were so jealous. Of course you'd have thought that Bernadette would be the worst when it came to being jealous—I mean, what with her being so pretty herself and all. But my sister didn't have a mean or jealous bone in her body. And I believe Starr Stubbs really liked her—sort of felt a kinship to her even, if you know what I mean, what with them both being so beautiful—even though she worked as the Stubbs' housekeeper up until she got too pregnant to work.

But I guess to say that Starr Stubbs felt a *kinship* to Bernadette is maybe not exactly right, now that I think about it. I mean, it seems like Starr liked my sister alright, but in that way that white people generally seem to like Indians—you know, sort of in a look-down-their-nose way. It's like in those shows you see on TV where this man owns a big plantation and always acts like he really loves his colored slaves, but still you can tell that he owns them and means for them to keep in their place or else he'll sell them or whip them. Well, that's sort of the way Starr Stubbs treats all the people around here.

I don't know, maybe it's just because she's rich and married to a famous singer—she might treat ever'body that way, even people back in New York City. I just know that there's always this uncomfortable feeling whenever you're around Starr Stubbs, like maybe you aren't as good as her. At least that's the way it seems to me, anyway.

You could always tell when Starr Stubbs was in town on account of that big Suburban of hers. It was black and the windows were black, too, so that you couldn't see if anybody was inside of there or not. I don't know if who-ever was inside could see out, but they must've been able to or else how could they drive around? And the license tag on that thing was a black and white one from Texas even though I never could understand why it wasn't from New Mexico like all the other license tags around here ex-cept for the ones on the BIA cars and trucks, and they had official U.S. government tags. Bernadette said it was be-cause Rounder Stubbs did a lot of his business in Texas and that Texas was his legal address—at least somewhere in Texas was. But it never did make sense to me, what with him and Starr having that great big house and all.

And another thing, even though she owned all those boots and high-heels, it seemed like Starr Stubbs wouldn't ever *walk* anywhere—even when it was nice weather. I've seen her stand and watch while one of the boys from over at the grocery store loaded maybe one little bag of stuff into the back end of her big Suburban because she wouldn't carry it out herself, and then she'd climb up in and start the motor and back out and drive over to the bank which is right next to the store. I mean, it isn't even ten feet away, I don't think. And every time she got in and out of that thing, she locked all the doors up with her keys, too. I believe I'd have just parked in one place and walked, if it was me.

The main trouble was, I think, that Starr Stubbs got real bored sometimes. And I don't just mean whenever her husband Rounder was out of town on one of his personal appearances, either. Bernadette said it was because Starr didn't really want to live clear out here—that she thought this place was nowhere and she missed the big city life she'd had when she was a model. She'd overheard Starr saying stuff like that to Rounder, and Starr had even talked to her about it a couple of times. You know, asking Bernadette what in the world kept her here and didn't she want to go live somewhere that was more alive, like even maybe Albuquerque. I think Bernadette really felt sorry for Starr, because she was so unhappy most of the time. She didn't seem to have any friends or family who came and visited her from New York City. And she sure didn't have what you'd call friends from around here, even though she probably could have had if she'd tried to be a little nicer to people. And to tell the truth, I don't think she was all that crazy about her husband, either.

The reason I say that is because there was sometimes trouble up there—the kind of trouble that comes when somebody gets to drinking too much and acting all crazy-like. Like the time Bernadette told me that Starr Stubbs had got real mad at her husband because he'd been foolin' around outside with their horses all one afternoon and drinking beer and probably other things and kept coming in and out of the door and tracking mud and horse shit all over the house when Bernadette had just mopped and vacuumed the whole place real good. And Starr had kept asking him to cut it out and then *telling* him and when he finally pushed her to the limit she got really mad and screamed and yelled at him and called him a shitass and a jerk and told Bernadette to come with her, that they didn't have to keep cleaning up after no shit-eating pig. And they got in Starr's big Suburban and drove over to Chama and just messed around for a couple of hours and then Starr bought them both a nice dinner at one of the tourist courts over there while she cooled down. Except that when they got back to the house the car that Rounder Stubbs usually drove was gone and there was a note stuck on the door that said STARR—NOW THE FUCKING HOUSE IS WASHED REAL GOOD DOES THAT MAKE YOU HAPPY? YOUR HUSBAND ROUNDER and when they walked in the front door everything was soaking wet because Rounder had took and run a garden hose with a lawn sprinkler attachment in through a window and set it right in the middle of the living room floor and turned it on full force before he left. It was pumping and spraying water everywhere. I guess a whole lot of stuff was ruined and Rounder Stubbs didn't come back home for something like a week after that. I don't know what went on when he finally did come home, either. But me, I wouldn't have wanted to be within a hundred miles of there whenever he did.

Anyway, after that there were some times whenever Rounder'd go out of town and Starr Stubbs would get all dressed up and get in her Suburban and drive over to Chama or down to Taos or Santa Fe, even, and then stay away for sometimes two or maybe three nights. Not that that proves there was any hanky-panky going on of course, but on more than one occasion, she'd go off and then come back with some guy who'd stay over. I can remember the first time that happened, Bernadette showed up a little before nine in the morning for work like usual and let herself into the kitchen. Well, she said that she hadn't even hung up her coat before Starr came charging out of the bedroom pulling on a bathrobe and lookin' like something the cat had drug in with her hair all messed up and talking all slurred and everything, and told Bernadette that she forgot to tell her that she wouldn't be needing her that day. And then she stood right there over her smoking cigarettes one after the other and watched while Bernadette called up Benjamin Begay on the telephone and got him to come to our house and get me since we didn't have no telephone so that I could go pick her up because Daddy had just dropped her off on his way to work and couldn't leave till lunchtime. Bernadette told me she believed she'd have had to walk back to town if I hadn't showed up when I did 'cause Starr was acting so antsy and all. It was pretty plain that there was somebody hiding out in the bedroom and that Starr Stubbs didn't want my sister to know about it.

I think Starr must've kinda embarrassed even herself that time, though, because after that whenever there was some hanky-panky going on up there she always just told Bernadette that a "gentleman was visiting from out of town" and let it go at that. I figure she must've known that Bernadette wouldn't make any trouble.

I remember we used to laugh a lot about that way of putting it—about her saying "a gentleman from out of town." I even got to where I used to tease Bernadette sometimes by referring to Anderson George as that "gentleman from out of town." But I wouldn't even tease her no more if Bernadette was here now.

I miss her so bad.

Like I was saying, Starr Stubbs was really just bored with everything, I think. And the one thing I've noticed that happens lots of times when people're bored and don't have nothin' to do is that they're apt to start drinking too much. And Starr Stubbs was no different than a lot of people.

Bernadette wasn't what you'd call a nosey kind of person, but she used to keep a count on the number of empty bottles she took out to the trash when she first got there to the big house in the morning. Not every day, of course, but sometimes she told me that she figured there must have been a whole bunch of "gentlemens from out of town" the night before because of there bein' two or three empty tequila and schnapps bottles. That's what Starr Stubbs drank, tequila mixed with peppermint schnapps—she called it a "Mexican Blizzard"—and Bernadette said it wasn't unusual to see her sitting there in her book room with her nose stuck in some book about Indians and sipping on one of those things at nine in the morning, some days.

Rounder Stubbs, he drank Wild Turkey. But he also did coke—and I don't mean the kind that comes from the store, either. I figure that he must not have thought any of us around here had enough sense to know what that stuff was, since he never made no effort to hide the fact that he would sit around at the big dining room table with a mirror and razor blade making neat little white lines of the white powder that he would then sniff up into his nose through a straw or something. And it wasn't just when he had company, either. Though usually anybody who came to visit would join Rounder at the dining room table. In most homes visitors get offered coffee or Pepsi or maybe a beer—but then maybe that's just around here where people don't have much money, I don't know.

Bernadette said that one time when he noticed she was watching him he just grinned up at her real big.

"Now Bernadette, don't you go mentioning to anybody that you saw me doing this, you hear? It's just that if I don't get my occasional dose of nose candy I can't hardly even think straight."

Then he sucked some more of the white powder up into his nose.

"Now, I understand lots of you Indians chew on them peyote cactus-button-mood-elevators 'cause they give you visions," he said. "Ain't that right? Hell-fire, Bernadette, it's the same thing . . . it's just that this here stuff is the medicine some of us white folks use for *our* visions."

Then Rounder nodded back toward the biggest bedroom where his wife, as usual, was spending her morning putting on her makeup and listening to real loud music on the stereo.

"Now, Mrs. Stubbs in there, she's what a lot of folks'd call a real serious visionary," he said. "It's just that she gets her visions in all kinds of different ways—mostly from tequila bottles and them little red pills she gets from the brown UPS delivery truck that drives up here direct from New York City. But then I don't imagine she'd be averse to chewin' on no cactus, neither—least ways not if she thought it'd make her feel good."

The mud and snow treads on the tires of the black and silver pickup made a loud whine as they rolled steadily over the dry pavement alongside the broken yellow line of U.S. 666.

Stretching north into the black night from Gallup toward Shiprock, the road was as familiar to the two brothers in the pickup as any road could be. They'd made this trip together any number of times for as long as either could remember. The main north-south passage across the eastern edge of the vast Navajo Reservation, it claimed almost as many Indians as did State Road 44 between Cuba and Farmington.

The driver of the pickup sat straight and tall, his hands gripped firmly to the wheel, his dark eyes staring directly ahead a hundred yards or so to the place where the light from the truck's high beams faded into blackness. There was little traffic to be seen at two-thirty in the morning— an occasional semi hauling cattle or sheep or whatever else the big eighteen-wheelers carried—but Tom George was well aware that even though they were several miles from anything that could be remotely considered a town, or village even, there was always a good chance there'd be someone walking along the asphalt on his way to or from who knows where. Or there'd be sheep on the road. Or a cow.

"Anderson." He spoke the name softly, in case his brother was sleeping. "Hey, you awake?"

The other sat leaning against the passenger-side door. Tom could see by the faint glow from the instrument lights that his brother was bent slightly toward him, and that he held his left arm gingerly away from his side. He spoke softly in response.

"They need to bring in some softer dirt for that arena if they're gonna hold rodeos over there at Ganado," he said. "Anyway they ought to have the courtesy at least to pick up the bigger rocks and broken bottles if they expect this injun cowpoke to come all this way to ride their sorry-assed buckin' horses again."

Tom George smiled and shook his head. "*Try* to ride their buckin' horses, you mean. Man, oh, man—that scrufty little red nag you drew sure enough gave you fits . . . how long you figure you stayed on her, little brother? Maybe half a second out of the chute?"

Anderson George turned his head and looked sullenly at his brother. "And I suppose now you're gonna tell me I ought to take up goat ropin' like you and half the other candy-assed boys who ain't about to get their jeans dirty but still manage to find their way to every event within drivin' distance, huh?"

He turned back toward the window and ran his right hand gently over his bruised ribs.

"Ouch!" he winced sharply and then smiled to himself in the darkness of the truck.

"I guess maybe you're right, though," he mumbled. "I know Bernadette agrees with you—at least she does every time she sees me eat dirt or get stepped on."

Anderson adjusted the rolled up towel wedged in the hollow behind his back. He settled into the seat as comfortably as he could, and tipped his dusty black hat down over his eyes.

"Of course whenever I win a contest, don't neither one of you suggest I switch to barrel racin' or pole bendin', huh?"

"You winned a contest?" Tom said softly, grinning now. "I don't seem to recall that one—could it be I was absent from that particular rodeo?"

"Ah, hell. You just stick to your drivin' and keep quiet so I can get me some sleep. And watch out you don't run over no goats out here and end up gettin' us both killed. The New Mexico state highway department spends a lot of good money paying their thieves and murderers at the prison over in Santa Fe to paint up signs that warn us law-abiding motorists about all the LIVESTOCK XING out on these highways. Now if you'll just keep your eyes peeled for any of those stray livestocks that might be xing each other out in the middle of this road, I intend to get me some beauty rest."

"Oh, no you don't, little brother . . . I expect you to help keep me awake. Seems to me you're the one who's in such a big hurry to get to Dulce by morning . . . seems to me you're afraid some young buck will come along and steal your girlfriend while you're out of town."

"Now I told you Bernadette had to go to work and couldn't get off," Anderson pushed his hat back up off his eyes. "You know if she'd been able to get off, she'd have come along."

"Yeah, and then she woulda been there to see you eat some more of that Arizona dirt, too," Tom grinned.

"Well, at least I'd be gettin' some sympathy from Bernadette. Now let me alone, can't you see I'm injured?"

"You're all the time tellin' everybody that you're one tough Indian, so quit your whining. We're almost to Sheep Springs, maybe that fillin' station there is open. I could sure use some coffee right about now—maybe a sandwich."

Gracie

Bernadette said that she figured they'd be showin' up sometime before lunch, and that we ought to go ahead and get some of our chores done instead of just sitting around waiting for them.

And so she was busy in at the kitchen table folding the laundry she'd just brought in from the clothesline out at the side of the house when we both heard the sound of their pickup drive up in front and honk twice.

Even if we hadn't heard the horn honkin', we most likely would have still heard that silly dog of theirs that was staying with us yipping and barking all excited—like it was answering the honk from the truck. I guess that little dog had been listening for them to show up, same as us. I was in the front room ironing a pair of our Daddy's khaki work trousers and watching one of those game shows that involves dumb questions and loud buzzes and bells on that beat-up little black and white television set we have. It's a wonder we can see anything at all on that television set since it just has one of those cheap sets of rabbit ear antennas that wouldn't be any good at all except that Daddy put these little flags made out of tinfoil on each one of its ears. But we're still always having to adjust that antenna and fiddle with the knobs—at least with the knobs that aren't broken off, that is.

I hollered into the kitchen, "Hey, Bernadette! It's

Anderson . . . and Tom's with him, too."

Thinking back now, Bernadette probably smiled at hearing me say that. I mean, that was something that went without saying.

"I bet didn't neither one of them two win nothing down there at Arizona," I said over the noise from the television. "Seems to me like those guys'd spend their money on something other than rodeo entry fees and gas to go drivin' all over the place."

I could hear my sister rushing around in the kitchen. She was probably making sure that there weren't any of her underclothes out where the guys might see them. And knowing her, I imagine she glanced at her reflection in the hall mirror too, to make sure that her hair was in place before she went to the door and opened it. She didn't have to worry, of course—Bernadette's hair was always in place.

The guys had gotten out of their truck and were standing beside it in the mid-morning sun. Tom George had his hat in one hand while he stretched his back and shoulders that were stiff from sitting so long in that one position. Chaco, that's that little blue-heeler dog who heard the pickup even before me and Bernadette did, was leaping way up in the air in that clownish way he had of showing how much he missed those boys. They call that kind of dog a blue heeler because their fur is this mixture of black and gray and white hair that really does look blue. Bernadette probably kept care of and fed Chaco as much or maybe even more than Anderson or Tom did, and he'd leap and jump just as excitedly for anybody who showed him some attention, but he was really their dog.

I could see that Anderson was favoring his left side when he got down out of the pickup—he'd hurt his ribs or shoulder, I figured. Bernadette could see it, too. But she wasn't the kind to make any sort of a fuss—not in front of me and Tom, at least.

My sister pushed open the torn screen door and kind of nodded toward those two.

"Come into the house and I'll fix us some tea," she said. "Gracie'll turn off the television set and you can tell us about your trip. Are you guys hungry?"

Bernadette stood to the side and held the screen door for him so Tom George could come into the house. I can still remember how Tom put his hat back on as he came in the door. Anderson followed his brother inside and stopped at the door to wait for Bernadette to go in first. He used his foot to keep Chaco back from the door—he didn't kick him, really, but just sort of pushed the dog away with his boot.

"What happened, did you get hurt?" Bernadette asked, and she reached out toward his left arm.

Anderson shrugged. "It's nothin'," he said. "Just hit the ground a little too hard this time, is all. I told Tom that them Ganado boys over there sure need to get themselves some softer material to put down in their arena if they expect me to ride them rank old horses again," he smiled at my sister—it was easy to tell why she was crazy about him. "You should've seen 'em Bernadette—they didn't have nothin' but a pen full of killers is all. I mean, it was stock they'd bought or more than likely stole off trucks headed for the dog food factory—didn't matter which one you drew, neither, they's all bad news."

Bernadette went into the kitchen to mix up some instant iced tea for all of us. I unplugged the iron and folded up the ironing board and leaned it against the wall. When I didn't turn off the television set, Tom and Anderson sat down next to each other on the couch and stared at the snowy picture of the game show.

I should tell you that our house didn't have much furniture in it—at least not as much as some people like those Stubbs out on the highway have. The one old couch that we had was all broken-down and me and Bernadette had tried to cover it up with this mustard-colored cotton bedspread that we weren't using at the time. And there was stains from lilac hair oil on the back of the couch from where our Daddy sat and watched television or took naps. We had two wooden ladder-back chairs that were pushed up against the wall next to the couch so that four or maybe five people at most could sit in the room at one time. We didn't have any coffee table, or end tables or no lamps. And the room just had that one single light up in the ceiling. The nicest thing in the room was this real tall buffet where we kept some of our good stuff. Stuff like some matching drinking glasses with colorful pictures of horses on them, and a pretty pink vase with some plastic roses, and some glass figurines—animals, mostly, like deer and cats. And on one shelf, next to the white Bible that the church people gave us once when they came by to visit, we had some nice pictures in picture frames. One showed Bernadette in a white graduating cap and gown. I think that one was taken on the same day she graduated from the BIA high school down in Santa Fe. Another one was cut out from the pages of the newspaper, and it showed Bernadette dancing the fancy shawl dance at some powwow somewhere—probably in Oklahoma, I don't really know. The paper had started to turn yellow, but the person who took that picture was a real good photographer and had caught Bernadette at exactly the right second. Under the picture there was a caption that said: DULCE APACHE GIRL TAKES FIRST PLACE. There were other pictures, too—mostly school pictures of me and Bernadette, and a small faded picture of our mother back when she was still alive, and one that showed Daddy when he was a young man looking real serious in his Marine Corps uniform.

The floors in all the rooms of our house were made

out of linoleum. And the linoleum was this kind of gray-green pattern that was supposed to look like carpet, I guess. But it just looked like linoleum to me. On the wall in the front room there were these two pictures in real fancy gold frames. In the biggest one there was a painting that showed this Indian guy who wasn't wearing nothing but a breech cloth and a feather war bonnet, sitting up on this spotted horse of his with his arms spread wide apart looking up at the sky, probably at the "Great Spirit." In the other frame, which was my favorite one, was this picture of Jesus . . . you know, with the light shining on him just right and a halo real pretty around his hair, and with him standing there right in the middle of a flock of these really white, clean sheep, and him holding a baby lamb in his arms and looking down at it. It was real pretty. There wasn't no glass in either one of those picture frames.

I sat down on one of the wooden chairs against the wall, under the picture of Jesus.

"Did you guys get to go and look around in that Hubbell's trading post over there at Ganado?" I asked. "I got to go there once with Daddy . . . it's one of my most favorite places."

Just then Bernadette came back in from the kitchen and handed each of the boys a tall glass of tea with lots of sugar in it. I remember there was just one ice cube floating in each glass. We only had one ice tray that didn't leak and lots of times somebody would take ice out and then forget to fill that tray back up with water—forget or else be too lazy. Bernadette usually blamed it on me whenever that happened, but I know for a fact she was guilty of doing it sometimes herself.

I guess she'd heard me ask about Ganado and thought I was bein' too inquisitive or something.

"They went to ride in the rodeo, Gracie—they weren't on a shopping trip, you know." Then Bernadette walked over and switched off the television set.

"Anyway," she said, "It looks to me like Anderson got hurt and he certainly doesn't need to have you pesterin' him if he's hurt."

Then before Anderson could say anything I noticed Tom winked at my sister and me.

"Aw, don't worry," he said. "He didn't take much of a fall. Heck, if he'd stayed on that booger more'n about a half-second, they'd have maybe at least cleared the chute and then he wouldn't have landed on the fence and broke no board. I tell you, them Ganado boys ain't gonna allow Anderson to enter any more of their rodeos what with the way he's always bustin' up their corrals and puttin' big dents in their arena dirt.

"Besides, you know us Navajos are too proud and stoic to show it when we have pain and injury." He had his hand up in front of his mouth so that we wouldn't be able to see his crooked teeth when he smiled real big at saying all this.

And Anderson George, he just sat there on that mustard-colored couch and acted all shy and embarrassed—staring down at the toes of his boots. I believe he knew that Bernadette was feeling sorry for him and that's exactly what he wanted and I probably added to it by asking did he really break the fence?

"Yeah," was all that he said. I honestly believe that he was hoping to make me and especially Bernadette feel sorry for him.

Starr

Except for Bernadette, I didn't have any friends in Dulce.

Rounder used to remind me that Bernadette was my housekeeper:

"*Jesus*, Starr," he'd say. "You pay out good money for Bernadette to come over here every day and pretend to be cleanin' up the house when it's spotless already. She's your housekeeper, for chrissakes—it just ain't seemly that my wife would count her Indian housekeeper as her best friend."

"Why, I do believe you're serious, aren't you?" I was annoyed that my husband—who could be such a hick most of the time—could and would put on such airs at other times.

"I'll remind you Mr. Country & Western Singing Star, that Ike Danley and the guys in White Trash are on *your* fucking payroll, but still you count them as your closest drinkin' buddies. As a matter of fact," I continued to rub it in, "I do believe those are not just your closest, but your only buddies."

But I know that Bernadette really was my friend.

Bernadette Lefthand was one of the most beautiful people I've ever known. Certainly she had the blackest, shiniest hair and eyes that I've ever seen on a human. On the other hand, Bernadette was, I think, painfully shy. But then maybe that's just the way Indians act around white people, I can never really decide.

Like when I'd happen to see Bernadette at the town's only grocery store, or at the bank or the post office. At those times it seemed almost as though Bernadette didn't know me—even if we passed in an aisle or were standing beside one another in line, Bernadette wouldn't so much as acknowledge me, rather she'd make a clear effort not even to make eye contact with me. It's true that if I spoke to Bernadette first, she'd stop and visit, but I felt like she always was somehow uncomfortable in doing so. At first I felt hurt, thinking it was because Bernadette didn't want her Indian friends to see her talking to a white woman. Later on there was a period when I was convinced that all that was simply an indication of Bernadette's shyness. Finally though, I reached the conclusion that Bernadette's attitude toward me in public was the result of some learned response that these Indians have toward whites. It's as though they don't want to risk being snubbed and so don't speak unless they're spoken to first.

On the other hand, I truly believe Bernadette loved the time she spent in my house. I remember how sometimes we'd spend hours just talking. I had become fascinated with Indian cultures and I used to tell her about things I'd been reading and ask what she thought about this or that. I'm afraid that like most white people, I'd always thought of Indians as though they were all alike. I guess you could say I'd been the perfect little pupil in school when it came to learning about Columbus "discovering" America and the cannibals that he found there and the myth about "Custer's Last Stand" and the Indian Wars—all the things that they used to teach as if they were true when in fact they weren't. Some of my fondest memories are of those long, lazy afternoons spent talking with Bernadette—the look I'd see in her eyes when I'd tell her about the lies they told in my school, about the awful truths that I'd discovered only as a grown-up. Of course she didn't know a lot of those things and I think she enjoyed hearing about them as much as I did.

Sometimes she would tell me something about her family—when I first knew her she lived at home with her father and sister, her mother was dead—and occasionally she would tell me stories about her boyfriend and his brother. Sometimes I used to ask Bernadette to go with me when I went to Santa Fe or Albuquerque to go shopping, and even though she always acted like she was just going along to help out in that way that a maid might help her employer, I believe she actually enjoyed those trips as much as anything we ever did. And later on, when she got married and had her baby, Bernadette asked me to be the child's godmother, which I took to be a great honor even though I'm not a religious person and don't really even know what a godmother is supposed to do.

At the time, Rounder had said that Bernadette only asked because we had more money than anybody she knew.

"See there," he said. "That just shows that your Bernadette's as smart as she is pretty. She knows damn well that by making you her kid's godmother it'll get big expensive presents at Christmastime and on its birthdays. How do you think these Indians up here would have gotten by for so long if it wasn't for the fact that they've developed a talent for making rich white people feel halfway sorry for them?"

Later, after Bernadette was killed, I can't help but believe Rounder regretted saying those things. At least I know he'd get anxious any time Bernadette's name would come up or something happened that might remind him of her. Like when somebody would come to the house to visit who'd been there before and didn't know what had happened and would ask if that good-looking Indian girl was still working for us and then act truly sad when they heard why she wasn't.

It seemed like everyone loved Bernadette—there was just something about her that was magic.

I don't care what Rounder or anybody else says, Bernadette was my friend.

When I first knew Bernadette, she was living at home with her father and younger sister and just going with Anderson—I don't know why, but dating doesn't seem like the right word to use.

Anderson was this really tall and gorgeous Navajo kid from over in Arizona—Window Rock, I believe it was, or maybe Chinle . . . anyway it was one of those dreary little Navajo reservation towns. I guess Bernadette and Anderson met when they both were going to high school in Santa Fe. A lot of the Indian kids go to school in Santa Fe because of the fact that reservation schools are so bad and because people live so scattered out around this country.

I remember I first saw Anderson and his brother once when Rounder needed to hire some help to work on fences. He'd asked Bernadette on a Friday to send around any of the local guys who wanted some work the next week and only those two showed up. As it turned out, they were far and away the best workers we were ever able to find around there but they both had regular jobs in the oil fields somewhere and they'd shown up to help out mostly as a favor to Bernadette, who probably didn't want to be embarrassed by maybe having nobody show up at all or seeming to be able to get only some of the regular town good-for-nothings when Rounder had given her the responsibility of finding some reliable workers.

Then later, when Bernadette and Anderson got married and moved into that godawful little trailer house in town, I used to see him around quite a bit. After awhile he just stopped going to the oil fields much at all. I never really understood if the work had run out or what he did for a job or if he even had a job at all, but he'd bring Bernadette up to the house and then pick her up most days, and sometimes I'd get him to help me work with the horses. Bernadette was very proud of the fact that Anderson rode in rodeos in the summertime, and she had let me know early on that he was an excellent hand with horses.

Bernadette was right. When it came to horses— whether it was riding them or training them or even doctoring them—I honestly don't think there was anything that Anderson didn't know. Trouble was, he got to drinking too much.

I have to admit that I honestly believe there's a great deal of truth to that old thing about how Indians can't drink whiskey. It's just that simple. I don't know exactly *why* that is and I'm aware that lots of the people Rounder always refers to as knee-jerk liberals maintain that that's only a stereotype image that bigoted white people hold about Indians. But I believe it's true anyway. They really *can't* hold their liquor. I read once in the Albuquerque newspaper, in an article about the alcohol problem on the Navajo reservation, that at least part of the reason they have such trouble with liquor is that since it's illegal to have booze on the reservation in the first place, that if you have some whiskey or wine, the best thing you can do is to drink it straight down right away so that you can get rid of the bottle and not take a chance on getting caught with the evidence.

There was that, and then there was something about how Indians, even when they are drinking socially, haven't got a clue as to when or how to stop. That is, as a people they can't seem to just have one or two drinks, rather they keep on drinking until finally they can't drink anymore because they've lost the coordination it takes to lift the bottle to their mouths. I don't remember if it was some supposed expert who wrote that article, or if it was based on any kind of scientific research or not. The fact of the matter is, however, that no matter what the reason, Indians can't drink, and I know it.

Which is why I feel like I should never have offered Anderson George a drink that afternoon after we'd been working at halter-breaking one of the colts. Not that there was any problem then, you understand—he didn't overdo or anything. It's just that it established a pattern. It was like it made it okay for Anderson to come in the house and have a drink after he'd helped with the horses or while he was waiting for Bernadette to finish up with whatever she was doing.

After all, Anderson George *was* Bernadette's husband. And he was always polite. And he was gorgeous. I didn't think there was any harm.

"Can I offer you something, Anderson . . . a beer, maybe, or some wine?"

He looked embarrassed for a moment. Then he nodded. "If you got some whiskey I'd take a little drink of that."

So I poured a highball glass half full of Jack Daniels.

"Water?"

"No."

"Bernadette brags that you're quite a rodeo cowboy," I said. "Tell me about riding in a rodeo. I'm afraid my experience with rodeos has been mainly during intermissions when my husband played at Houston and one time at Madison Square Garden in New York."

"Nothin' much to tell," he said. "I contest saddle

broncs at the all-Indian rodeos, mainly. They don't have no intermissions at those rodeos except maybe after somebody's got throwed down and stomped on and they got to hold things up till they can get the guy loaded up in a pickup and take him off to the clinic."

I noticed that Anderson's glass was empty, and I was surprised because I hadn't seen him take a drink.

"I heard that your brother was a calf roper." As soon as I'd said it I realized I shouldn't have. Anderson acted like he hadn't heard me and I remember that he reached out his hand and touched the wall—it was as if he were steadying himself.

"Yeah."

I was about to pour him another drink when Bernadette came into the room. She smiled at me and then looked hard at the glass on the table in front of her husband.

Anderson stood up abruptly and walked to the door.

"You shouldn't oughta work that colt too much for a couple days," he said, looking at me. "Just maybe five minutes at a time so he don't forget what he's learned so far. And you ought not to feed him so much of that sweet feed, neither. He's gettin' fat and sassy and you don't want him gettin' too rammy on you—he'll hurt himself or maybe you.

"Or worse, he might even hurt *me*," he grinned.

And they left.

Bernadette never mentioned anything to me about Anderson drinking that day, or any of the other times. But I couldn't help but feel guilty . . . like I was somehow at least partly to blame for what happened later.

And Bernadette didn't tell me that she was pregnant right away, either.

In fact, I'd started to tease her sometimes that she was

maybe dipping into the fry bread a little too much—that married life was beginning to show on her already—stuff like that. I really shouldn't have been surprised when Bernadette told me one morning that she and Anderson were going to have a baby.

Certainly the last thing in the world that *I* ever wanted was to get pregnant. So being the self-centered bitch that I am, it was difficult for me to imagine that anyone could actually want a child.

"Oh, I'm sorry, Bernadette!" I said.

The expression on her face told me that Bernadette was confused by my reaction. Of course, she would be.

"I mean, I'm very happy for you . . . if that's what you want—a baby, that is." Now I was confused, too, it seemed.

"It's just that I'm a little surprised, that's all—I didn't know you were planning a family."

What a dumb ass I was for saying that—I could have kicked myself. I'm sure the concept of planning a family never entered Bernadette's mind. In Bernadette's world it seemed natural that when a girl got married she had babies.

Period.

I made a conscious effort over the next few months to appear excited for Bernadette. Any time I was in a book shop in Santa Fe I'd pick up some baby books to take back to her. I might have even appeared too excited. At least Rounder thought so.

"Goddammit, Starr," he told me. "The way you do carry on over that baby you'd think it was you who's pregnant."

"Don't even joke like that, Stubbs!" I shrieked. "I just want her to feel good about what's coming. Thank God it's her and not me."

It got to the point where I could tell if Anderson had

been drinking when he came to pick up Bernadette by whether or not he got out of his pickup.

The first time I can remember noticing was once when he drove up and then just sat there in the driveway for about twenty minutes—he didn't honk or go up to the door. I knew Bernadette hadn't seen him sitting out there and so I called to him from the porch to come on up to the house.

But he just sat there so I went out to see about him.

Even though he had the window rolled down just a crack, I could still smell the strong odor of whiskey on his breath and see that his eyes were red and watery.

It seemed like more and more often he stayed in the truck. There were times, in fact, when Anderson didn't show up at all. Sometimes Gracie, Bernadette's sister, would come instead. Or their father. And once Dee—the nutty woman who owns the cafe in town and who they rented that awful little trailer from—showed up. It was clear on those days that Bernadette was upset, even though she tried not to show it.

"I haven't seen Anderson in a while," I said to her one day when I noticed Bernadette watching the driveway, waiting for someone to come for her. "Is everything going okay at your house?"

"Oh, sure," Bernadette answered. "It's just that he's not been feelin' too perky lately. He worries a lot, you know—about the baby comin' and money and stuff."

"Well, you tell him that I really could use some help with those horses out there—tell him they've gotten pretty rowdy since he's not coming around so much anymore.

"And tell him I'll pay him for coming, too," I added. "He should know that I will, but you tell him anyway."

"I'll tell him," Bernadette said.

Just then Gracie Lefthand drove up in their father's

old blue Ford.

I can still remember how deep and dark and how terribly sad Bernadette's eyes could look sometimes. Thinking back now, I believe that was the first moment that I'd really noticed that sad look of hers, though. It still breaks my heart to remember.

"See you tomorrow," Bernadette said.

And then she smiled at me before she turned and stepped off the porch and walked toward the waiting truck.

There are various sources of evil in the Navajo view of the cosmos, but the worst of these pertains to sorcery and witchcraft.

—Marc Simmons
Witchcraft in the Southwest (1974)

Gracie

Bernadette had a friend who was from Hopi over in Arizona named Mae Lomayaktewa, and she lived at Shongopovi Village on Second Mesa.

Bernadette had met her at school, and they liked each other right off the bat. I remember one time Mae came and stayed with us for a few days during one of their vacations from school—I believe it was Thanksgiving, which is kind of a funny holiday for Indians to celebrate, I'd say. I figure probably that Mae didn't have enough time or money to go to her own home and didn't want to stay around the dormitory with some of the others who didn't get to go to their homes neither. Anyway, she came to Dulce and her and Bernadette just messed around and went down to Taos to visit at Aunt Lupe's place. And I guess Mae wasn't used to the weather being so cold like it can get down there. Bernadette said that she just about froze to death and never did get over it and that anytime anybody would even mention Taos, Mae would go to exclaiming all about how cold it is down there.

It was funny, but they told me that at Taos when Bernadette introduced Mae around to some of the people there that this one real old man who used to be the war chief a long time ago and was an important member of the tribal council reached out with both his hands and rubbed and touched Mae all over her face and hair and shoulders real gentle-like and then he cupped his hands over his mouth and nose and breathed in real deep. Aunt Lupe said that the old man was real religious in the old Indian ways and that he did that to take some of Mae's strength and power and to breath it into his own body. Not to be mean, or evil, but because he knew that the Hopi are a very powerful and ancient people and that him doing that really showed a lot of respect for Mae. I don't know, I thought it was kinda creepy myself—like by doing that he was stealing part of her strength and she would just naturally be weaker because of him doing it. But Aunt Lupe said that wasn't so.

I really liked meeting those different people from all the different places. Which is why I think Bernadette was real lucky that she got to go to that school over in Santa Fe and then got to go around to visit places where she had friends.

I was thinking about Mae Lomayaktewa because that was one friend of Bernadette's that I did get to go visit one time when Bernadette and Anderson and Tom George went and took me along on the trip.

It was during the summer before Bernadette and Anderson got married and there was supposed to be two rodeos going on over in Arizona that Anderson wanted to ride in and the guys said that they could manage to hit them both and that it would be a good chance to go stay at Hopi and visit with Mae and did Bernadette and me want to come along too. Well, Bernadette sure did and I wasn't about to miss the chance to go on a big adventure like that, and Daddy said it would be okay and we went in the boys' pickup.

You probably realize that a pickup truck is just not real comfortable for four people to ride up in front, even though you see Navajos stuffing five or six grown-ups in their trucks all the time. But Tom and Anderson had that

good camper shell on their truck and there was this sliding glass window between the camper and the front seat
so that even though I rode most of that trip in back with
the saddles and Chaco, I could still hear what all was
going on and talk to them and pass up cold pop from the
ice chest that we had along whenever somebody got
thirsty. It was a real fun trip for me—maybe even the best
thing that I ever got to do.

I remember we loaded up and left on a Thursday. It
was pretty hot, but we had plenty of cold pop that we got
at the grocery store in Dulce and some cookies and stuff.

One thing, Tom George never would allow anybody
to drink beer in that truck. He said that was a rule because
nothing smelled worse than old stale beer when people
spilled it on the seatcovers which they always did, it
seemed like. But I really think that he made up that rule
because he didn't want Anderson drinkin' while they were
on the road. Not that I'd ever noticed Anderson drinking
all that much back then, but I figure Tom knew better
than anybody else about Anderson's tendencies.

The road between Dulce and Farmington is just real
boring and because we had all of us made that drive so
much, everything always looked real plain. We didn't even
stop in Farmington for nothing, but went right on
through to Shiprock. Tom kidded me and Bernadette
then by telling us that once we passed Shiprock we were
really on the Navajo Reservation—he just called it the
"Rez"—and he figured two handsome local boys like him
and Anderson could maybe trade a couple of bad-tem-
pered Apache women for something really valuable, like
maybe a goat or some plastic beads. I laughed at that and
Bernadette pretended to smack him on his arm. Then
Anderson took up the joke and said that he heard that the
trader up ahead at Mexican Water wasn't one of them
Arabs that had taken over most of the trading posts, espe-

cially those out on the interstate and in the bigger towns like Gallup and Scottsdale, Arizona, and that he'd heard that this guy was always on the lookout for good-looking Apache women, but that they'd probably have to wait till they got to Many Farms to get rid of such ugly ones. So after that, for the next few miles, whenever we'd pass by some guy walking along the road, Bernadette would holler back to me about how handsome that guy looked and then ask Tom to stop and pick them up next time there was two of them—one for her and one for me. But of course it was only a matter of time before Tom called her bluff by slowing way down and pretending that he was going to stop when we came up to these two really scuzzy-looking white guys with bedrolls and half-gallon plastic water jugs.

After that Bernadette quit talking so big about picking up hitchhikers.

We got some sandwiches at Mexican Water and me and Bernadette looked around in the store while Tom filled the pickup with gas and Anderson let Chaco run around and smell tires while he checked the oil and cleaned the bugs off the glass. Then we headed on out. The guys said that they figured we could eat supper and maybe stay overnight at their grandmother's place at Chinle. I was hoping we'd have time to look around in Canyon de Chelly which was right there at Chinle since I'd only seen it in pictures and Anderson had told me once about his grandmother having a place in there where she kept some of her sheep in the summertime. When I asked him about it Anderson said that if we ended up staying the night that we'd probably have to sleep in his grandmother's hogan up in the canyon because their main house wasn't all that big. I said that would suit me just fine and Bernadette said it would suit her, too.

I didn't know about those others, but I can tell you

that I was having a real fine time and we hadn't even got to where we were going to yet.

I'd always heard people say the name Many Farms and I knew that it was a town in Arizona. Of course I had a picture in my head of it being a nice neat community with a lot of nice white fences and green pastures where the many farmers who lived around there grew vegetables and stuff. Boy was I wrong.

The first thing I noticed when we started getting close to Many Farms was that the barbed wire fences were just about covered with those white plastic bags that you get at the grocery store ever since they quit using brown paper sacks that you could burn. I guess people throw those white bags away and then the wind gets them and carries them across the land until they get snagged on a fence or a cactus bush or something. Actually, those plastic bags are white and red. The red is the writing on them that says, "Basha's." Tom told us that Basha's is the name of a lot of the grocery stores in Arizona and on the Navajo Reservation—that they're kinda like an Indian Safeway. I found out when we went into a couple of them later on that they're really nice big stores and have everything you'd need to buy and even a kind of a bakery-type place where they sell stuff for lunches and things. But I mean to tell you their plastic bags have sure ruined the looks of the country—at least around Many Farms, Arizona, they have.

And another thing I noticed was all the horses that were turned out on the road and were eating the grass next to the highway the closer we got to Chinle. I don't think I ever saw so many horses turned out on the road-way—it's a wonder to me that they don't all get hit by cars and trucks. Bernadette was noticing it too because she said something about all the horses. Tom laughed and said that whenever people around there talked about it they always joked and said they were "Justin's horses." He said Justin was a Navajo guy who rented out horses to tourists to ride in Canyon de Chelly and that he had lots of horses.

Most tourists don't ride horses, of course. Tom said that most of them who want to go into the canyon ride on these big green army-looking things with six wheels that won't get stuck in the sand that the Indians call "Shake and Bakes" because they ride real rough and bouncy and in the summer it can get god-awful hot down in there. But the tourists still pay money to go on the half- or all-day trips. Tom said that since white people seem to like to write their names everywhere and take souvenirs home with them even if they know they aren't supposed to, that they aren't allowed in Canyon de Chelly without a Navajo guide to keep an eye on them.

Even before we drove up to where Anderson's grandparents lived he had warned us that they were real attached to the old ways and that we better not be expecting any indoor toilets or running water or other fancy things like we were used to at home. I remember thinking it was funny that Anderson would feel like we were used to fancy things at our house, which I always thought of as bein' real plain. I guess it just goes to show that it all depends on how you look at a place.

So when Tom George pulled off the pavement and drove out across this real bare-looking country and kept bouncing across this rough dirt road for what seemed like twenty minutes, we weren't too surprised. At least I wasn't. And then we finally came up to this round house that turned out to be a Navajo hogan built out of logs and with mud filling up the cracks and just one door that I could see and one window. There was a kind of oily looking black smoke coming out of a stovepipe right in the middle of the dirt roof.

Tom honked the horn on the pickup and said that here we were.

There was an old, gray pickup parked there beside the hogan and there was an even older, skinny brown horse with a saddle on it standing there tied to a scrubby little bush beside the pickup. The horse was sleeping, or at least it was standing there with its eyes closed and its bottom lip hanging way down like horses do and it always looks to me like they're sleeping. Not very far from the house was a pen made out of crooked juniper limbs and inside of the pen there was a bunch of sheep and another horse. A scruffy looking yellow dog came trotting up to our truck and started peeing on the tires before Tom even had a chance to come to a complete stop. The door of the hogan was open and even though it was in the shade and I could barely see because the sun was so bright in my eyes, it looked to me like a woman who I figured must be the grandmother was standing in the door looking at us. She had a stick in her hand and when she recognized that it was her grandsons in the truck, she walked out into the sun and started shooing the dog away.

The old woman was wearing a long, full skirt that brushed the dirt, and a dark purple velvet shirt with a beautiful big silver and leather concho belt and turquoise bracelets and big round needlepoint turquoise pins like you see Navajo women wearing in pictures but just think that they got all dressed up for the picture but they didn't after all. And when that big skirt moved in a certain way, you could see that she was wearing a pair of high-top black tennis shoes with holes in the part that is made out of cloth. I just thought that was sort of unusual—that a traditional Navajo woman would be wearing sneakers.

Tom spoke to his grandmother in the Navajo language which me and Bernadette didn't understand, of course, and to tell the truth I was kind of surprised to hear Tom talk it because I didn't know *he* understood it either. But of course he would, just like Bernadette and me understand our Apache language although I don't talk it too good.

When Tom spoke to her, his grandmother nodded and said something back to him. Then she raised her hand and pointed toward where Anderson had gotten down out of the truck and come around to open the tailgate so me and Chaco could get out. Of course that yellow dog didn't especially take to havin' a stranger invade his territory and so him and Chaco had to spend a couple of minutes sniffing each other and acting all macho. Anderson stood shading his eyes. He smiled and nodded to his grandmother. That was all the greeting that was exchanged as far as I could tell.

Then Bernadette climbed down out of the truck and spoke in English. "Hello, Grandmother." The old woman smiled when she recognized my sister.

"Oh, it's Bernadette Lefthand," she said. "I'm happy to see you."

Bernadette walked over and shook the old woman's hand. Then she turned toward where I was standing.

"Grandmother," she said. "This girl is my sister, her name is Gracie Lefthand. She lives at my father's house in Dulce. She doesn't attend the school in Santa Fe yet, but maybe she will next year."

"Gracie's a very pretty name," the old woman said, looking me up and down. Except when she said the word it was like she was saying "*purr*-dy." Then she reached out and shook my hand very formal-like.

"I'm glad to meet you, Mrs. George," I said.

Bernadette told me then that she was pretty deaf and that I should call her "Grandmother" to be polite.

So I said again, louder this time, "I'm happy to know

you, Grandmother." And then, just to make some conversation I asked, "Is this your sleepy horse?"

I guess I still wasn't talking loud enough because then Tom said something to her in their language and she put her hand over her mouth and giggled.

She looked at the horse and then at me, still with her hand to her mouth and laughing. "No, that's not my horse, child," she said. "That's just one of Justin's horses that I rented from him for today to go and gather up those sheeps in that corral."

For a second there I wasn't really sure if they were kidding me or what, but when I looked over at Anderson and Bernadette, I could see that both of them and the grandmother thought this was a big joke. So I smiled at her to show that I could enjoy it, too—even if I didn't understand what was so funny. I guessed it was just a Navajo thing.

The next thing I knew there was this very tall, thin old man wearing a dusty black flat-brimmed hat standing there beside Tom George. I hadn't seen him come up and since the country around that place was so flat and bare, I guess he must have maybe been inside the hogan and just come out quietly while we were talking about the horse. I remember noticing that this man wore a pair of large, teardrop-shaped turquoise earrings that hung from wire loops through his ears and that they were obviously real old and heavy since the holes where his ears had been pierced were pretty big—actually they were more like slits. And he wore a medicine pouch on his belt, something that you don't see too often anymore and as a matter of fact, makes a lot of people nervous when they do see one. To be honest, it makes Navajo people more than just nervous since it seems like most of them are afraid of the old people who carry medicine pouches—afraid they have witch medicine in there. But I guess the grandfather was pretty famous around the Chinle area as a singer—that is, as a medicine man—which is something I don't really understand too much except that those kind of men have a lot of power and you better treat them good or else you might be sorry. Besides that I was struck by the way that his proud face was wrinkled but still handsome and looked enough like an older Anderson George so that you could tell where that boy had got his good looks.

Tom was talking to his grandfather in Navajo and it was plain he was talking to him about Bernadette and me even though I couldn't understand the language. Bernadette had told me that the grandfather didn't speak any English, which I thought was pretty strange since I know a lot of young Indians who don't speak their own language but only English. Sometimes the older people at Dulce and down at Taos might not talk it too good, but most of them that I knew about could speak English when they had to.

Later on we ate mutton stew and frybread that the grandmother cooked on a wood fire out by the sheep pen even though there was a big, black iron stove inside the hogan. Anderson got the ice chest out of the pickup and we had Pepsis and orange pop which I guess was a pretty big treat for the grandfather since he drank three of the orange pops. Then while the grandmother showed us a real nice rug that she'd been working on that she said she'd sell at Crown Point in the fall, the guys and their grandfather looked at the sheep in the pen while the old man rolled cigarettes from a can of Bugler tobacco and smoked them one after the other. To tell the truth, I think he was just real happy to see his grandsons. They didn't talk all that much, but I think he was glad just to have them around.

As it ended up, we didn't get to stay in the summer hogan in Canyon de Chelly after all because one of the grandmother's sisters or something was using that place in exchange for watching some of her goats for her.

Instead, after Tom and Anderson had visited with their grandfather and checked out the place, Tom said did we want to take a drive and at least see the canyon since we were so close by. Well of course I did and Bernadette did too, and so we all climbed in the pickup and rode over to take a look. All except the grandmother who I guess had to stay home to watch the sheep. Anyway she didn't go along, but the old man rode up in the front with the guys and Bernadette sat in the back with me and Chaco.

Since the George family had a place in there and we were all Indians and the Park Service rangers can't tell a Navajo from an Apache, we were able to drive right past the entrance and into the canyon where tourists aren't allowed to go. The floor of the canyon is actually a riverbed that is real wide and since there's only a small amount of water most of the year it makes a pretty good road that you can drive on. Tom told us that there's some bad spots where there's apt to be quicksand and so he was watchin' carefully where he steered and his grandfather would every now and then point out a spot that Tom would then maneuver around to keep from getting stuck. Those quicksand spots didn't look particularly different to me. What I mean is, I couldn't see that they looked any different from any other part of the riverbed, but Bernadette said that we'd really be in trouble if we happened to get stuck and that the old man could tell just by looking and that it wasn't a case of memorizing where the quicksand was either, but that the dangerous thing about it is that quicksand shifts around and one day a place that's been solid just all of a sudden turns into sand soup. Man, I'm just glad they didn't any of them ask *me* to drive. Not that they would have of course, but still I wouldn't want to have all that worry on my mind.

If you haven't ever seen the Canyon de Chelly, let me tell you it's a sight to see all right. The sides of the canyon walls are this kind of pink rock with dark streaks that climb straight up for what I figure must be hundreds and hundreds of feet in most places and then there are all these big groves of trees and areas of nice green grass down there in the bottom with cows and horses and of course sheep grazing—it's just real beautiful. Also there are lots of old ruins here and there on the walls, that are cliff dwellings where the old ones lived a long time ago. And there are even hogans where people stay now, like the one Anderson and Tom's grandmother owns. Also there's a lot of important history connected to the canyon. Tom says that Kit Carson, who white people like to pretend is some kind of big hero, marched into the canyon about a hundred years ago with an army and burned down all the Navajos' peach trees and corn fields. After which he rounded up the people and took them off to some fort or prison somewhere off in New Mexico. Anderson said that looking around at all the beauty you could see how come the white government didn't want no Indians living there—it was just too gorgeous to waste on Indians, he said.

While we rode along the old grandfather kept pointing things out and talking to Tom and Anderson who would then tell me and Bernadette what he was saying. Like he showed us some drawings on the sides of the cliffs and would every once in awhile point out a ruin that we wouldn't never have spotted if it hadn't been for him showing us.

It seemed like we drove quite a ways back into there until we came to a spot where Tom stopped and we all got out and stretched our legs and looked around. This was a place they called Standing Cow Ruin and it was just a real nice spot we thought. They called the place that on

account of the fact that there was an old drawing way up
on the cliff wall that looked like a cow standing there.

While we were walking around we noticed that there
was a falling-down rock hogan back in among some trees
that me and Bernadette were fixing to go over and look at
until the old man started talking sort of excited-like to
Tom and frowning and motioning us away.

Tom told us his grandfather was saying that this was a
very bad place—that this particular hogan was a bad place.
He said that it was where somebody or other had died
once and so wouldn't nobody ever live or even go near
there again. He told us not to even walk over there.

I know this, if there's anything that these Navajo people don't like even one little bit, it's dead bodies.

Not that very many people who aren't Navajos like
dead bodies either, of course. But most other people aren't
as completely weird about dead people as that bunch of
Indians. I mean, they ain't any more scared of dying than
most, but dead folks is really a big thing with them.

Like for instance, if somebody who's a Navajo is real
sickly and it looks like maybe they aren't long for this
world, their family will try and find a place away from the
house for that person to stay at up until the time they
die—like a white people's hospital if there's one around.
The reason is, that if a person dies inside the house—or in
the case of Navajos, inside the *hogan*—then won't nobody
live in that place anymore because of the ghost of that
dead person hangin' around, which I guess was the case in
that falling-down hogan in the canyon. I should probably
tell you that instead of saying *ghost*, though, Navajos say
chindi, which means ghost—or like some people say, it can
also mean *witch*.

And another thing Navajos don't do is talk about dead
people. The main reason they don't is because they believe that if you say a dead person's name that the ghost,

or *chindi*, of that person will think that you're calling it and will come and pester you and probably you'll catch whatever it was that caused that person to die in the first place. Even Navajos that have lived a long time around white people and have gone to white schools and who you wouldn't think would be too superstitious about things usually believe in all that kinda stuff.

It seems kind of complicated, I know, but you know how whenever you drive around places where there's lots of Indians one of the first things you notice—right after how many beer cans and wine bottles there are beside the road, that is—that one thing you notice is how many churches and missions there are scattered around those places? How it seems like lots of times there's more white missionaries than there are Indians on some of the reservations? Well, my Daddy told me that that's because white people get off on converting us heathen Indians over to their particular brand of religion—they get points or something, he figured. Of course my family is all Catholics. Daddy bein' Pueblo he did both ways, Catholic and old way Indian, but whenever there was regular type religious things going on like Christmas or Easter it was mostly Catholic stuff around our house.

But like I was saying, the Navajo Reservation is no exception to the rule about all the different missionaries hanging around there competing with each other to see who can sign up the most natives. And what with the Navajo Reservation being the biggest one around, naturally there's about every kind of church you can imagine out there in every kind of building you can think of— there's even some in old, beat-up house trailers. Of course the problem with all of this is, that since Navajos are so terrible scared of dead people and since white missionaries are constantly preaching to the people about how things are gonna get a whole lot better when they die and even going around plastering pictures of Jesus mysteriously rising up outta the grave everywhere and singing songs promising that He's gonna come back from the dead so as to make everybody's life better and . . . well, you see what I mean, don't you?

That kinda stuff just doesn't make a lotta sense to Navajo people.

And another thing a Navajo won't talk about is witches and witchcraft. No sir, they're real, real scared of witches, that's for darned sure. But probably not any more scared than Pueblos are, I don't think. In fact, they say that Navajos are pretty scared of Pueblos even, because they believe the Pueblos have stronger witch powers than them. Me, I just always try not to think too much about any of that creepy kinda stuff. And like I said, Navajos don't ever talk about it on account of they figure people will think you *are* a witch if you seem to know very much about them.

I can tell you this, though, I know for a fact there are witches and that they can do terrible bad things to people, especially if people don't protect themselves and keep their eye out for them.

Lucky for us there's lots of ways you can tell if there's a witch around, though—like if your dogs start barking real loud at night, or there's a bad wind, or a coyote follows you when you're out walking. And by the way, if a coyote does follow you, they say that it means your brother or your sister is going to die, but that you shouldn't try to shoot the coyote because he's just trying to warn you and he don't intend to harm you.

No coyote ever followed me anywhere, by the way. At least not as far as I know about. But my sister still died anyway.

And also a lot of the older Navajo people believe that

if you get a disease that the *hataali* can't cure with chants, then that's a sure enough sign that you've been witched. But then that's mainly just old people who don't understand about cancer and AIDS and some of the other diseases that white people brought with them. The *hataali*— that's what Navajo people call their medicine men or singers—they can help out with most natural sicknesses and problems, but they usually can't do much good when it comes to those white-caused things.

I found out that lots of Navajos keep secret stuff around their houses to ward off evil—like different medicines and things. And by "medicine" I don't mean like aspirin or Pepto Bismol—I mean *Indian*-type medicine. But mainly they say you shouldn't ever go around at night because that's when bad things are lurking around and all kinds of evil can get done to you.

But no matter what, the most important thing of all, a lot of people say, is that you don't never speak the private name of yourself or anybody in your family or any of your friends when you're around strangers or people that you don't trust. See, a witch has got to know a person's secret name—what Indian people call our "war" name—before it can work any evil on that person. So just don't ever do it.

Well, of course we didn't go near the ruin after hearing how the grandfather was warning us. I can tell you one other thing, you might not always understand exactly why it is that some people feel certain ways about things, but you better not go against those feelings. Not if you know what's good for you, anyway.

It was getting late and would be dark before too long so Anderson said we'd better start back. We had all climbed back into the truck except that I noticed the grandfather hadn't gotten in but was just standin' there beside the open door.

The old man was standing very still and I could see that he was holding real tight onto that leather medicine pouch that I'd seen hanging on his belt back at his place. I remember how he was just standing there motionless and staring up at the rim of the canyon and how his face looked very pale and how it seemed to me like he was mumbling something to himself real low . . . or maybe it wasn't really mumbling, but that his breathing was all of a sudden getting heavy and rasping-like. I looked up and tried to see what it was he was staring at but couldn't make out anything. Whatever it was he saw or whatever it was in his mind, all I know is it caused me to shiver and I could feel goosebumps startin' to rise up on my back and on my neck like it was all of a sudden getting cold and it wasn't. I remember looking to see if anybody else was experiencing this creepy feeling, but it didn't seem like they were. Except for Chaco. That dog was just quivering and kind of cowering in the corner of the pickup bed like maybe he figured he was about to get whipped or at least scolded for something. And a strange thing was how his nose was twitching like maybe there was some terrible smell that only he could smell. It was spooky, is what it was.

But then the old man seemed to snap out of it and turned around and got in and shut the door hard and started rolling himself a cigarette and jabbering somethin' in Navajo that caused the boys to laugh and Tom started the truck and we went bouncing off across the sand and headed for the entrance to the canyon.

▼▼▼

The whole of the rugged canyon floor below him now lay in deep shadow. He stood precariously close to the sheer edge of the cliff, high on the canyon's rim where the last orange rays of the setting sun reflected off his mirrored sunglasses.

He counted five of them far below in the shadows. Yet even from so high above them and in the darkness of the shadows he could make out that three of the tiny figures wore black hats and that the dog was with them . . . that blue dog. The black and silver pickup seemed little more than a toy from this height, and the figures of the people were like insects. Still, he knew who they were. Knew that one of them was her. And he gazed directly at the setting sun and began to chant softly:

"Yu! On high you repose great bird, there at the far distant place. Now you have arisen at once and come down. You have alighted midway between them where they two are standing. You have spoiled their souls immediately. They have at once become separated."

He sensed that one of the black hats carried powerful medicine . . . that it felt his presence there above . . . that it knew he was watching . . . that it felt his power. He shifted his gaze to the people below and continued the chant:

"I am a strong man; I stand at the sunset. This woman is of the feather people, she is called Tompaxemu. We shall instantly turn her soul over. We shall turn it over as we go toward the darkness. I am a strong man. Here where I stand her soul has attached itself to mine. Let her eyes in their sockets be forever watching for me. There can be no loneliness where my body is."

Now there was a painful ringing in his ears and a sharp bile rose up in his throat. He put a hand to his head and hacked up vile phlegm which he then spit into the dust at his feet. And wiping a misshapen hand across his mouth, he watched as the last black hat finally climbed into the truck below and he saw the tiny vehicle drive away. He coughed and spit again, and then, turning away from the canyon, he limped toward the battered, green pickup.

As he turned the ignition key he smiled to himself and spoke aloud.

"Morning Rain."

▼▼▼

Oh, but that was a fun time—it was a real adventure, is what it was.

Because their hogan was pretty small, once we got back to the grandparents' place me and Bernadette made us a bed in the back of the pickup and the boys put bedrolls down on the ground over by the sheep pen. The weather was nice so there wasn't any problem with that arrangement even though I had been kind of looking forward to staying in a hogan back in the canyon. Bernadette told me before we went to sleep though that maybe on the way back after the trip to Hopi and the rodeos we could stop by again. I said I hoped so.

But we didn't.

I remember how the next morning it was just barely even light and there was this terrible commotion that scared me half to death and made me sit straight up and nearly bump my head before I even knew where in the world I was at.

The old man was pounding his hands on the side of that camper shell and laughing and hollering something that of course I couldn't understand. And all that commotion got that Chaco dog excited and he was running around and barking to beat the band and the grandparents' yellow dog, who it turned out was happy to have some dog company to visit with for a change, joined in at the top of his lungs. Bernadette must have already been awake because she was laughing too and at the same time telling me to settle down and not get startled. She said that the old man had already greeted the morning sun as was the Navajo custom and why their doors were always on the east side of the hogans and that now he was just greeting us. I looked out the window of the camper and saw that Tom and Anderson were sitting there on a bench

that was beside the door of the hogan, drinking hot coffee
and grinning at what their grandfather was doing.

"Grandfather says that Apache girls are lazy," Anderson was saying. "He says Navajo women would have already made a good fire and fixed some food and taken the
sheep to get water by this time."

"You tell your grandfather that he scared Gracie so bad
that she might not ever come visit him again!" Bernadette
said.

By this time I was awake enough to see what all was
happening and I'd got to giggling at the grandfather who
was peering in the window right next to my head and grinning real big and showing that even though he was a handsome man with his mouth closed, he was missing quite a
few of his teeth and what teeth there were left were brown-
and yellow-looking from all the cigarettes he smoked.

"Up and at 'em," Tom hollered. "Let's get this show
on the road . . . there's some rodeo prize money with
Anderson George's name on it waiting for us over at
Piñon!"

I know I felt kind of weird and uneasy around him for
some reason, but I believe that the old man really did like
me and Bernadette, because he kept smiling and pointing
at us and saying things to Tom and Anderson all the time
while we were standing by the truck and drinking coffee
and eating the mutton ribs that Grandmother had
cooked for us before she got up on that skinny brown
horse and said good-bye and rode off to take the sheep
out for the day.

And when we were loaded up and ready to leave, the
old man came up to each of us and put his hands on our
shoulders and looked right into our faces and gave this
pretty long speech. I remember thinking that he looked
especially sad when he was talking to Tom, like maybe he
knew he wouldn't be seein' that boy for a long time or

maybe even ever again. And I noticed that he stared at Anderson with a real funny look in his eyes and that Anderson looked almost scared at whatever it was the old man was saying when he spoke to him. Later on, though, Anderson told me that all the old man's talkin' was really just a traditional blessing that we would be safe from evil things and that we'd continue to walk in beauty which he said is important to the Navajo Way.

The road between Chinle and Piñon, Arizona, is not usually very busy, at least that's what Tom says. But this rodeo in Piñon and the doin's that just naturally go along with any rodeo was attracting lots of Indian people from Many Farms and Chinle and places like that so there were quite a few pickups filled with families and pulling horse trailers and there was hitchhikers on the road.

I'd been expecting that Piñon would be a town something like Dulce. I mean, Anderson said it was a little place, but he didn't say it was just a trading post and gas station out in the middle of nowhere. When we got there, there was already lots of pickup trucks parked all around the trading post and there was probably about a hundred Indian people hanging around on the porch and all around out front visiting and eating potato chips and Fritos and stuff and drinking cans of pop and smoking cigarettes and spitting tobacco. And from the way all the women, or at least the older women that is, were all dressed up fit to kill in their long skirts and velvet blouses and big silver and turquoise jewelry, I guessed this was a pretty special event. And sure enough I noticed right off that the men were all wearing those black cowboy hats they're so fond of.

Daddy says that them black hats are the main cause of a lot of Navajo men being so dumb—of course he didn't say that whenever Anderson and Tom was around so as not to hurt their feelings or cause Bernadette to get all huffy. Anyway, he says that those black felt hats cook their brains in the summer and he never was able to understand why Navajos don't just switch over to straw hats which are sure cheap enough and stay cooler in the summertime. Daddy says even white people got enough sense to do that.

Tom parked the truck and Bernadette came around to let Chaco and me out of the back and we all went into the trading post to look around and see about where you signed up for the rodeo events. Of course the store wasn't as big as the one back home, and it wasn't a Basha's, but it had a lot of the same stuff in it. Except that it was a real trading post where people could pawn jewelry and rifles and rugs and things like that for money or at least for credit. In fact, there was a rug room that they kept locked up where if a person was interested in maybe buying a rug the white man who ran the place would get the key and take them inside and show them around. And there was a big glass case filled with fancy pawn jewelry—some of it for sale and some just waiting for the person who pawned it to come and bail it out. And there was clothes and all kinds of supplies for livestock as well as canned tomatoes and other vegetables and a refrigerated section with fresh meat most of which was sheep, and ice cream bars and even frozen TV dinners.

Since it was lunchtime, me and Bernadette got some sandwiches and chips from a woman working at the food counter. I got a plain cheese sandwich and Bernadette had the special "Navajo Burger" which I figure was probably not even made out of cow meat like most burgers since those Navajo people are so partial to their sheep. And of course we also got us each a Pepsi. Anyway, then we stood in line to pay while Anderson and Tom talked to the trader, Mr. McGee, about Anderson riding in the rodeo. I was wondering if the store was always this busy or if it was just on account of the rodeo when I noticed that most of the women who were buying food were paying for it with coupons that they had in brown government envelopes and I realized that it was the first of the month and the WIC coupons had probably just come in the mail. I'm pretty sure everybody in there knew we were tourists on account of they could see we were using cash money— that and the fact that we were Apaches and not Navajos or Hopis. Indians can tell you know.

When Anderson had got all signed up and paid his entry fee, we went out behind the store to where the arena and the holding pens were so that we could look at the rough stock, which is what they call the horses and the bulls that rodeo cowboys ride.

Like I said, Anderson contested in the saddle bronc riding, which just means that he got to use a saddle when he tried to ride a bucking horse instead of just being perched up there bareback with nothing but one handle to hold onto. Not that using a saddle makes it any easier to ride a good bucking horse—at least that's what Anderson told me, and I figure he should know.

And in case you're wondering about Tom George and why he didn't sign up too, it was because if he did anything at a rodeo it was to enter the calf roping and to do that you have to have your own horse to ride that you take around with you to the different rodeos. And even though Tom did have a real good roping horse back at his uncle's place outside of Window Rock, he didn't have the horse with him on this particular trip.

While we stood around out there looking at the animals, Tom said that according to McGee, the rodeo was supposed to start at two o'clock and they were supposed to hold the drawing to see which animal the cowboys had to ride at about one or one-thirty. Naturally, all of this was based on "Indian Time" which just means that it was anybody's guess when stuff would really happen.

While the guys were looking over the horses and talking with some fellows they knew from other rodeos, me and Bernadette wandered around looking at where some people had set up these tables and were selling things. The fact that this was the day people got their assistance checks, added to the way a rodeo is just naturally such a big social event, meant that it was a good day and place to try and sell stuff. For instance there was some ladies with piles of used clothes and toys for sale and there was this man who had some real nice beadwork and some silver rings and earrings that he'd made. And then on the back end of a brown pickup these other two women had set up a Coleman stove and were busy making frybread and coffee that they would sell you for a dollar—that's a dollar for a big frybread and a styrofoam cup of hot, strong coffee. And of course that included honey or salt for your frybread if you wanted it. One thing I'll say about Navajo people, they sure do know how to make good frybread and it's one of my favorite things—something I can't hardly ever resist when it's around. And you can bet it'll be around if there's any kind of Indian doin's going on at all.

One of the people that Anderson and Tom was talking to over by the holding pens was this guy by the name of Emmett Take Horse.

He was Navajo, and lived somewhere up around Many Farms I think, and had gone to school with them and Bernadette over at Santa Fe. I found out later that he was a clan brother to Anderson and Tom. The thing is, in the Navajo Way a person has to always be polite and hospitable to a person from their clan—it's almost like you're

actually *related* to the person who's your clan brother—
and this means they can't be turned away from your home
if they need food or even money. Tom and Anderson were
of the Bitter-Water clan on their mother's side and the
Salt clan on their father's side—"Bitter-Water born for
Salt" was how Tom put it. Emmett Take Horse was
Bitter-Water born for Honey-Combed-Rock-People, and
so you see they were clan brothers. Later on, whenever I
had trouble understanding why Anderson would want to
have anything to do with Emmett, I just had to remember
the clan connection.

I remember I recognized having seen him hanging
around before in different places by the way that his right
leg was all kind of twisted up so that he walked with a bad
limp and the fact that his hand on that same side was
scarred up pretty bad and he was missin' a couple of fingers.

Bernadette told me later that back at the school there
had been some rumors goin' around that this Emmett
Take Horse was involved with the bad side of the Navajo
Way. Some of the kids she knew even hinted around that
he was a witch. And like I said, a lot of Indians and almost
all Navajos are very serious in their belief that there really
are witches. And not just back in the old days, either, they
believe there are witches walking around today. And when
I say witches, I'm not talkin' about the kind you see in
pictures around Halloween, either. If there's one thing
you can say for sure about Navajo people, it's that there's
just a whole lot of evil in the world according to their way
of thinking. And if you want to know what is the worst
thing they have to put up with, well, it's witches is what it
is. This is not something you should take lightly. If you're
ever going to understand those people, the most important thing you have to remember is that to a Navajo just
living in the world is a dangerous thing.

Bernadette told me that a real strong belief to Navajos

is that you better not torment a person that even *might* be a witch, because if it turns out the person isn't one, just the fact that you've suspected them is a terrible thing and that's bad. And of course, if the person *is* a witch and you make him mad you're *really* in for it. It's peculiar, I know, but it works out that witches wind up getting treated pretty good on account of everybody's too scared to rub them the wrong way. Bernadette said that she really figured that all the gossip about Emmett Take Horse was mainly on account of him being scarred up so bad and that some of the people at the school thought he looked pitiful and so made him out to be evil and ugly. That's just the way some people can be, you know—kind of cruel whenever somebody's different from them. And like I said, Navajos see danger all around anyway and so it stands to reason that somebody who looks or acts different will just naturally arouse suspicion.

Another thing, Bernadette said that this Emmett guy used to sometimes try and get her to go out with him—at first, anyway, before it got to be so obvious to everybody that her and Anderson were pretty much a steady couple. It wasn't my sister's nature to be in the least bit cruel to anybody and I figure that she was probably nicer to Emmett Take Horse than anybody else at that school, but then I guess it was sort of hard to get him to take no for an answer and she said she'd finally had to get pretty firm with him and then there must've also been some words or something between him and Anderson George at one point—Bernadette didn't say all that much about it so I imagine it wasn't nothing serious, though.

It seems like Emmett Take Horse had been a pretty good horse rider back before he got cut up so bad in this crazy kind of an accident and he was well-known all over as a good person to ride your horse in a match race.

Match races, in case you aren't familiar with them, are

where two guys will get in a big argument over whose horse is the fastest and to settle a bet they'll go to where there is a place that they can race to find out once and for all who's the winner. Lots of times there'll be a pretty good crowd there watching too, and a lot of betting goes on over what will be the outcome. Anyway, one of the important parts of the strategy of match racing is figuring out who you'll get to ride your horse in the race since it just naturally figures that a good rider who is also not too big and fat will give the advantage to one horse over the other as long as they're otherwise pretty evenly matched. So you see, Emmett Take Horse was short and skinny and certainly not scared of going all out, and so he was a popular jockey and if you didn't know too much about the horses that were racing and you wanted to bet anyway, you were dumb if you bet against any horse that Emmett Take Horse was riding. Anyway that's what Bernadette said and she didn't just make things up.

So what they do in a match race is, they put the two horses in starting gates just like at the state fair races over in Albuquerque, but instead of there being ten or twelve horses there are just these two. And they have a certain distance—like maybe a half of a mile—that somebody's already measured off with their pickup speedometer and that's where the finish line is marked and somebody who's supposed to be honest stands down there in case the horses come across neck and neck and they have to get an opinion on which one is the winner.

Most of the time these match race courses are either situated out in the middle of nowhere and the jockeys are in charge of seeing that the horses run a straight line, or else some men have lined the course with bales of hay or something else that isn't going to cause too much commotion if somebody's sorry horse decides he don't want to run in no straight line—which happens a lot I guess.

But listen to this . . . Bernadette says that there's this one match race track over by Many Farms where whoever it was that built it just got it lined with two barbed wire fences strung out for the whole distance on each side of where the horses run! I mean, they have real starting gates like you'd want to see and everything, but then the track is lined on each side by this fence made out of three or four strands of barbed wire strung on iron posts that's stretched out for the whole length of the race track!

So you've probably already figured out what it was that happened to Emmett Take Horse and how it is he came to have got himself so terrible crippled and scarred up.

Of course Bernadette didn't actually see what happened that day, but she said that she heard all about it from people who did see it—who saw how the horse that Emmett was riding in this particular race had been a little bit behind the other one at first and how he was gaining on it and that just as he started to pass him about halfway down the track the other guy steered his horse over to the right so that he was crowding Emmett over toward the barbed wire fence on that side of the track. I guess it's pretty common for that to happen, as it turns out—that to help make sure they'd win a race on that particular track some of the guys would every once in a while push the other guy over toward the fence so that the one being pushed would most usually chicken out and slow his horse down so as not to get too close to that barbed wire.

Wouldn't you know it though, that fellow Emmett Take Horse called the other guy's bluff that day. And I guess it's just real lucky for him that he's even alive today.

People who were there say that Emmett's horse was practically flying down that race track when it leaned clear over to within a inch of the wire to keep from being bumped and that it just still kept right on running and that the rusty barbs on that wire cut first through the bluejeans Emmett Take Horse was wearin' and then through his skin and then his muscle and then even sawed halfway through his legbone in just like a part of a second before he could manage to get his hand down and try to grab ahold of that wire. And they say that he nearly tore his hand off doing it, too—grabbing at that sharp wire and trying to keep it from cutting his leg clean off.

The people who saw what all happened say it was just real gruesome and that the whole bunch that was out there that day all went about half-crazy when they seen what all was happening. Like you would imagine, there was just a whole lot of blood spurting everywhere—even before you could figure out what was happening there was this crazy amount of blood all over the place. They say it was like one second ever'body was standing around watching the race just as natural as you please, and then the next second there was this awful commotion at the fence with blood everywhere and that horse that Emmett Take Horse was riding on going not just halfway crazy but plumb insane and screaming like horses sometimes do and going all frantic from the smell of that hot blood and Emmett himself trying to get away from the fence and not really even understanding what all was happening to him, just knowing that something was terrible wrong and not having the slightest idea of what that something was. They say that he told people later that he never felt any kind of pain—that it was more like it was happening to somebody else, somebody that wasn't him.

If you want to know the truth, I'm real glad I wasn't over there to see that stuff going on that day, and I'll bet Bernadette was glad she wasn't there, too, even though I never heard her come right out and say so.

Tom George wasn't there that day either by the way, but he says that Emmett Take Horse would have died for sure or at least lost his leg and maybe even his hand if it hadn't been for the fact that there was some El Paso Natural Gas line workers there who were watching the race instead of doing their job checking on the gas wells and the lines and stuff back over around Farmington. Luckily those guys had a powerful two-way radio in their truck and right away called somebody who was able to get a helicopter to come right to where they were in just a little while and take Emmett to the hospital . . . clear over to Flagstaff, I think.

I don't know who they decided would have won the race if it hadn't been for that wreck, but they say that somebody took his rifle out of his pickup and shot that horse Emmett Take Horse was riding. Not because of what all happened, of course—after all, it wasn't that horse's fault that he got pushed into no fence. They had to shoot him because of how he was cut up pretty bad himself and on top of which had got all crazy and frantic over the smell of all that blood.

And they also tell about that other jockey in the race that day—the one that actually caused the wreck to happen in the first place. They tell about how he got bad sick not very long after that—got so skinny and sick that he just wasted away and that nobody could ever say what was wrong with him and that he finally died from it. Bernadette said that Anderson had kidded Emmett one time by saying that maybe he put a curse on that guy for causing the big wreck in the first place. But I guess Emmett didn't think that was too funny.

And wouldn't you know it, they still use that same set-up at the race track over there—I mean, they still have barbed wire running down each side of that track. At least that's what Tom George said.

And by the way, when our Daddy heard that story he just said "Navajos are pretty slow learners, ain't they?"

And didn't nobody offer to say anything different—not even Bernadette.

The rodeo finally got started at about three o'clock, which is pretty good for Indian doin's—being just one hour late.

Tom had parked the pickup right up next to the arena fence so that me and Bernadette could sit on the hood and be pretty comfortable and still have a real good view of all the goings on. And even though we didn't have umbrellas like a lot of the Navajo women use to keep the sun off them, it really wasn't too hot that particular day. Which was good since Chaco liked to sit up as high as he could get and so he was perched up on top of the cab of the truck which as you know can get awful hot to the touch if the sun's been beating down on it. I swear, that dog was just watching like he was real interested in all that was going on, too.

This was a pretty fancy rodeo, considerin' that it was about a hundred miles from nowhere and that there wasn't nobody but Indians involved in it. They had a real honest-to-god loudspeaker system for the announcer to use and a record or a tape recording of the "Star Spangled Banner" or the national anthem—whichever one it is that starts off patriotic events like rodeos, I never can remember. And there was this girl who must've been the queen of this particular rodeo or something, and she came riding out real fast on her horse carrying an American flag and then she did a fancy sliding stop in the middle of the arena and then, just like that, a roman candle or some other kind of firework went shooting out of the end of the pole that the flag was on! It was neat, I'll tell you. I still don't know how they did that and how come it didn't scare that girl's horse silly when it went off—the firecracker flagpole, that is. It scared *me*, that's for sure.

Then they introduced the oldest war veteran in the audience or at least the guy who claimed to be the oldest veteran. I don't think he was all that old, to tell the truth—I suspect that he was the only one they could persuade to admit to being old. Navajos are real silly about some things, you know. But then I guess maybe there's a thing about getting old that rubs Indian people the wrong way more than most. If you look around you're not apt to see many gray-haired Indians and you won't see a bald Indian man hardly ever. At Taos me and Bernadette used to get pretty tickled over how the older ladies had most of them dyed their hair jet black and the old men, too, and also there was one old man who wore this really awful-looking wig with pigtails at all the events down there. I'll swear, that wig looked like he must've got it at some after Halloween going-out-of-business-sale somewhere.

Anyway, the announcer talked about half the time in Navajo and the rest of the time in English. And like most announcers that I've seen, he told some real corny jokes every now and then, too. One he told that I can still remember was, "How do Navajos tell you when it's time to go to bed?" The answer was, "Hit the hay." That caused a big laugh, but of course if you didn't know that a famous Navajo greeting is "*Yah-ta-hey*," you probably wouldn't have got the humor.

Even though Tom wasn't entered, we watched the calf roping anyway. I can tell you that Chaco really got excited when that was going on. Like I already said, he's the kind of dog that just naturally wants to chase cows and snap at their heels—which is why that kind of dog is called a "heeler," I guess. So whenever he would see one of those calves running past, especially with a guy on a horse chasing it, that little dog would get all hyper and act like he was gonna jump right in the arena and chase that calf himself. And I believe he would have, too, if only me and Bernadette wouldn't have kept laughing and telling him to "stay."

And then we watched the bareback riding and the steer wrestling. Emmett Take Horse came over from the pens where Tom was waiting with Anderson for the saddle bronc riding event and hung around with us awhile and explained what all was going on. Bernadette may have known, but I didn't.

A funny thing that I noticed was that Chaco didn't seem to like Emmett Take Horse one bit, which was really peculiar when you consider that Chaco liked just about everybody. But around this one person that dog sure did act strange. You know, stuff like growling real low deep down in his throat and not making eye contact with Emmett whenever he was around. Bernadette even swatted Chaco once or twice when he started acting up like that, but Emmett Take Horse told her not to worry and in fact—and I thought this was surprising—kind of scolded her by saying that you shouldn't never hit or kick a dog because, like some people, it might decide to get back at you later on. He said that Navajos believe that dogs have particularly strong powers and that they can do evil things.

And then they held the barrel races and I really liked watching the girls do that. The girl who won was only eight years old the announcer said, but man was she good—or maybe I should say her horse was good. At least that's what Emmett Take Horse told me. He kind of belittled the whole event and said that if it was riding a good enough horse, even a monkey could win the barrel race. I don't know, it looked pretty hard to me.

Then it was time for the saddle bronc riding and of course we were all rooting for Anderson to win. Tom said that Anderson had drawn an ornery horse and that we

shouldn't expect him to do very good. But then I figured
he was just saying that so we wouldn't get our hopes up
too high, and all.

As it turned out Tom was right after all. Because just
as soon as Anderson got about halfway settled in the saddle, before they even got the chance to open up the door
good and let it start bucking out in the arena where the
crowd could watch, that horse flipped over upside-down.
Everybody who was watching got all concerned until
Anderson got untangled from the wreck and came out
brushing himself off and the announcer said that we all
ought to give him a big hand since all he was gonna get
for his efforts today was a little applause.

Later on Tom George said it was just real lucky
Anderson didn't get bad hurt. Of course Tom said that to
me and Bernadette where Anderson couldn't hear. To
Anderson, Tom said something like "Apparently you
didn't learn all that much back at Ganado, little brother—
like how it's the cowboy who's supposed to ride the
horse, and not the other way around."

And even though Tom kidded him, naturally we all felt
bad because Anderson felt so bad. Not just because of the
entry fee being wasted, either, but also because there's
this rule that says if you don't get a fair chance to ride,
they have to let you try again and we felt like they should
have let Anderson try again. But some guy who they said
was an official told Anderson that the ride counted and
that he was disqualified from winnin' and naturally nobody argued with him. One reason why Anderson felt so
bad I think was on account of that me and Bernadette—
and mostly Bernadette—was there to see it.

Anyway, Anderson came over and sat with us on the
pickup for the rest of the events. They always hold the
bull riding event last of all on account of it's a favorite of
the people who are watching and they don't want you to

leave early and maybe not buy that last bottle of pop or some more of that frybread. Me, I never could understand how come somebody would be brave enough to get up there on top of a big mean bull with a big string of slobber hanging out of its mouth and ride it—or maybe it's that them that do are just too dumb to know any better, I don't know. It's very exciting, though, and I liked seeing who would win. By the way, the winner was this guy from over at Mexican Water who Emmett Take Horse said he was somehow related to—by clan or something—and who I guess was pretty well known as a bull rider since Anderson and Tom and Emmett had all predicted he was gonna win even before he did.

After the rodeo most of the people who were there went back up to the trading post and sat out on the big porch in the late afternoon shade and smoked cigarettes and drank pop and ate ice cream bars.

There were pickup trucks with horse trailers parked all over the place out front and people standing around visiting and dogs sniffing at each other and kids playing under the porch. It was just real nice and I enjoyed it. Different men kept coming up and shaking hands with Anderson and Tom and talking to them in their language—Tom told me and Bernadette that they were congratulating Anderson for riding in the rodeo even though he hadn't done so good. He said that Navajos are very serious about their rodeos and that they appreciate guys making a good effort even if they don't end up winning.

After awhile Tom said he figured we'd better hit the road and while he made sure that there was plenty of gasoline in the truck we stocked up on orange pop and Fritos and some Oreo cookies from in the store. Then we loaded in—me and Chaco in the back—and started off down this dirt road toward Hopi.

We were going to visit Bernadette's friend Mae Lomayaktewa at Second Mesa.

▼▼▼

In case you didn't know it, the Hopi Reservation is plopped down right smack dab in the middle of the Navajo Reservation. Don't ask me why, it's just the way the BIA or somebody like that planned it, I figure. Anyway, there's a lot of bad feelings and grudges between the Hopi and the Navajo people because of that, and they usually don't get along too good. Come to think of it, I guess you could say that a lot of different Indians don't have much use for Navajos for one reason or another. Of course like I already told you, in the case of Anderson and Tom George it seemed to be okay that they were Navajo.

I'd always heard that one way you can tell where you are when you're on the Hopi Reservation is by which of the three mesas you happen to be on. Mae Lomayaktewa lived on the middle, or Second, mesa.

From Piñon, where the rodeo was held, to Second Mesa is only about thirty miles but it seems like a lot farther because of the bumpy dirt road and all the real fine dust that comes up into your pickup truck through that crack by the tailgate, and especially if you happen to be riding in the back and that dust is coming up through the crack and covering you up like it was doing to me and you-know-who. I remember it was close to getting dark when we got to the Hopi Cultural Center—which is the place where the pavement starts up again.

The cultural center is where they've built a nice restaurant and a motel and some shops where you can buy postcards and the Hopi jewelry and the kachina dolls that some of the men carve and stuff like that. It was a busy time of year and there was quite a few people in the restaurant eating—Indians and tourists both. And you know usually in a case like that you better find someplace else to eat if you're an Indian because you ain't likely to get much service. But this girl who was wearing a traditional black Hopi dress took us to a booth and gave us menus right away.

When Bernadette asked the girl about if she knew her friend Mae, the girl told us yes she knew her and that Mae lived at the village just down the road and that her aunt lived there as a matter of fact and would fetch her for us. Then she went back to the desk while we looked at the menus. We ordered some coffee and apricot pie with ice cream on top while we waited for Mae Lomayaktewa to show up. Which she did pretty soon, along with her brother.

After we'd all greeted one another, Mae and her brother—his name was Henry—sat down at the booth with us to wait while we finished our coffee before they took us to their house where we would be stayin' the night.

Mae was a very nice person and I liked her a lot. She wasn't as heavy-set as a lot of Hopi girls seem to be, and she was real pretty—at least I think she was. I liked the way that Mae was always very considerate of her family and of other people and I think she loved her home as much as anybody I ever knew loved the place they were from. And I mention her loving her home because lots of people say that the Hopi country is about as ugly and dry and godforsaken as any place can possibly be. Another thing I always remember about Mae Lomayaktewa is her telling me one time that except for those years that she was living at the school in Santa Fe, she had watched the sun come up and go down every single day of her life from her house which was set out on the edge of a tall mesa. She told me that her grandmother—who I guess was quite old—always woke up very early in the morning and that once this grandmother of hers was up, everybody else might as well get up too since the old grandmother had a habit of banging things around and making a whole lot of noise. Of course Mae laughed when she told about it, so it was plain that she loved her grandmother very much even though she *was* an early riser.

"I'm so happy to see you guys," Mae was smiling when she said that. "And you decided to visit at a good time because tomorrow's gonna be *tikive*—the dance day.

"It's real special, too, because the men from our village are doing the *Tasapkachina*." She spoke directly to Anderson and Tom. "That's a Navajo kachina dance and you guys are gonna feel especially honored to get to see it.

"There's a whole bunch of cooking going on down at our house tonight. The women are gettin' the food ready for the big celebration tomorrow. Maybe you and Gracie can help cook up something special that Apaches and Navajos like to eat, Bernadette. Hopis eat lots of corn, you know, and my mom and my aunts have spent the last three days making *piki* bread."

Tom George laughed at that. "You know us, Mae, we're Navajos and Navajos like to eat anything, long as it's free," he said. "They say that to get all our people within a hundred miles together for a meeting all you got to do is set out some free food. . . . Navajos can just naturally smell chow cookin'."

"Yeah," my sister laughed. "Especially if somebody's cooking up sheep meat and frybread."

When we were through with drinking our coffee, Henry Lomayaktewa piled in the truck with Anderson and Tom and, of course, Chaco, and they went driving off to see where some of the men who weren't dancing the next day were cooking these big heaps of corn in an underground pit out in a field somewhere. The dancers didn't help in the roasting of the corn on account of they had to spend the night before the dance down in the kivas.

Me and Bernadette, we rode with Mae in her car to Shongopovi Village where the women were sure enough cooking up a storm, just like Mae had said.

The house that Mae and her family lived in was built out of rocks and mud and there wasn't any electricity or running water as far as I could tell. What there was, was several small children playing in a big room with a bed in it that was lit by just these old-timey gas lights. That is, there was children laughing and playing when we first went in the door—the children got very wide-eyed and quiet when they saw that Mae had strangers with her. Most Indian children are very shy. Then farther back in the house was a pretty big kitchen where about eight or eleven women were busy cooking stuff on a big propane stove, and I also noticed that a couple of those green, two-burner Coleman stoves were set up on a big table over to the side to handle the overflow. Mae told us to put our coats and anything else we had in this one room near the kitchen where there were two beds. She said that was where we could lie down and sleep if we got tired. She told us that the guys would be staying not at this house, but someplace else where Henry would take them after they got done checking out the men cooking up all that corn for the next day's doin's.

Boy howdy, though, back in there in that kitchen those Hopi women were cooking up lots of good-smelling stuff—big pots full of stews and red chiles and beans and *posole* and I don't know what all. But I do know this, that place may have been as hot as an oven from all the cooking, but it smelled so good in there I thought I was going to faint, and I wasn't even hungry, havin' just had that big piece of apricot pie with ice cream on it. I figure all the ladies who were gathered there in the kitchen must've been Mae's aunts and cousins mostly. Anyway, they all seemed to know Bernadette already and seemed real glad to see her. When I was introduced around they even gave me big hugs and acted like I was welcome there, too. I tell you, even though it was kind of hot from all that cooking, it felt good and homey in the Lomayaktewa's kitchen. I liked it in there.

And later on, when I got to yawning too much and didn't want to insult anybody by them thinking that I was bored with the goin's-on and so went in that other room to lie down and try to go to sleep for awhile, I can still remember how good and cozy it felt just to stretch out on that bed and to smell the wood burning stove and all that food cooking and to hear the sounds of those women's laughing and telling stories. It reminded me of what it was like at Christmas back home, except of course it was summertime.

It wasn't even light outside when I first heard the sound of the drum and the bells and rattles on the dancers.

I looked over and saw that my sister had been sleeping on the other bed and that she heard the sounds from the kachinas too and was stirring around.

"Hey Gracie," Bernadette whispered. "You awake? We better hurry up so we don't miss anything."

But just then Mae stuck her head into the room. She looked just the same as she had the night before so I figured maybe she hadn't ever gone to bed herself.

"You lazybone Lefthands goin' to sleep all day?" she laughed. "Don't worry, that isn't the real thing yet that you're hearin'. The dancers always go through their steps out there first one time without their masks on before dawn. It's not for the people to watch though, it's more like a last minute practice. But it won't be long now, so hurry up and come have some coffee and bread. Henry will be bringin' Tom and Anderson over here pretty soon."

We were sitting in the kitchen joking and visiting and drinking coffee with lots of milk in it when the guys did show up. I was braiding Bernadette's hair.

The Lomayaktewa's place was situated right on the main plaza of their village. So when those young boys who had been sent to watch out for the dancers came running into the house to tell us that they were coming, all we had to do was step out the door and we could stand right there or lean up against the wall of the house and watch. Or, if we wanted to, Mae told us we could climb this ladder that went up to the roof of the house and then we'd have an even better place to see everything that was going on.

And sure enough pretty soon those boys came running in all excited and giggling and we all went outside to watch the dance.

The first thing I saw coming was this one guy carrying a big drum and following behind him was this long line of kachina dancers all dressed pretty much alike in turquoise-colored masks with what was supposed to be these kinda like bird beaks sticking out from the middle of each mask but looking more to me like big yellow noses. On top of the masks there were eagle feathers and bright red hair and they all had collars around their necks made out of evergreen branches and they wore fancy silver bracelets and conchas and Navajo woven belts and they each had turtle shell-rattles tied onto their legs. And the dancers all carried a rattle in one hand and a sprig of spruce in the other. Later on, from up on top of the roof where I could see better, I counted ninety-seven dancers—and then there was the drummer and the headman, which made ninety-nine altogether.

In case you never were lucky enough to see them, I can tell you that these Hopis dance just wonderful. They were a lot better than most other dancers that I ever saw. Every one of these guys was exactly in step and never missed a beat. They sang real low and sometimes kind of grunted or made a kind of a hooting noise—you know, kind of like an owl might make—and dipped their shoulders down, and all in perfect time. They did four cycles of this particular dance, each time facing a different direction and it took about twenty or thirty minutes. Then they lined up again and walked back to a kiva where Mae said that they would rest for about twenty minutes and then come out and dance again. She told us that this dance lasts all day.

"These dancers will keep coming back to dance probably ten or twelve different times," she told us. "And you better be especially careful around noontime, 'cause that's when the clowns are most likely to show up."

I had heard that Hopi clowns were even meaner than the ones down at Taos Pueblo who throw little children into the river there, so Mae didn't have to tell *me* to be careful.

Sure enough, about the fifth time the dancers danced, there was all of a sudden this big commotion in the crowd of spectators over to one side and when I looked up I could see that six clowns were climbing up on a roof over there. The first thing I noticed was that these clowns weren't dressed up neat like clowns sometimes are, but instead they were wearing raggedy old cut-off bluejeans and tennis shoes and they had mud or paint or something smeared all over them—even in their hair. They were whooping and causing a big commotion and pestering people in the crowd, but the dancers just went on like nothing unusual was happening.

One thing you always have to remember when the

clowns are around or especially when they're near to where you're standing, is to not look directly at them or to act like you're scared of them, which of course you should be, knowing what all they sometimes do to people. Like one good example of how they can sometimes be nasty is that these particular clowns were up on a roof and they walked over and stood in a line and proceeded to pee over the side—and I mean right down on top of this bunch of people who just happened to be standing there by the wall watching the dance and minding their own business! Man oh man, I was glad that I wasn't standing down there by that wall!

Like you can probably imagine, I didn't get to enjoy a whole lot more of the dancing because I was worrying myself half to death over keeping one eye out for those clowns. One thing that was kind of funny, though, was that the clowns must have recognized immediately that Tom and Anderson were Navajos—and like I said, this was a Navajo kachina dance. Anyway, once they spotted Anderson and Tom they right away came over to where they were standing with Bernadette and me and Mae Lomayaktewa and her brother Henry and started having this big loud conversation that wasn't in Hopi or Navajo or English or any other language that made any sense and pointing at the guys. And then they took Tom and Anderson's black hats and took turns wearing them around for awhile—strutting and swaggering all around and acting foolish and at the same time pretending like they were Navajos. Then two of the clowns who was wearing the black hats at the time came running over and made Bernadette and Mae dance with them in the Navajo style of social dancing. Of course all the people who were watching got a big kick out of that. I can tell you that even I was laughing real hard, but of course I was awful glad it wasn't me they'd decided to dance with. Luckily they gave the hats back after they got tired of that and except for some dirt on them, they weren't banged up too bad.

Anderson and Tom were pretty good-natured about the whole thing—but then what else can you do when you're a visitor in somebody else's village?

Tikive is not just a dance day at Hopi, either. It's also a feast day and believe me, we feasted. I can't remember when I ever ate that much food in one day. And we visited a lot, too. We saw a whole lot of Indian people that we knew from other places—or I guess I should really say that Bernadette and Anderson and Tom saw people they knew from other places, me having not been all that many places before.

Emmett Take Horse showed up.

Which wasn't all that surprising since as you know we were planning to be going to another rodeo before we headed back for home—this one was being held over at Ganado again—and with rodeos being such big deals among Navajo people, it wasn't one bit unusual for a lot of the same people to be there. And it also wasn't any wonder for Emmett Take Horse to show up at the feast at Hopi on his way to Ganado, either. It was like Tom had told Mae when we first got there—if you want to attract Navajos, all you have to do is to put out some free food. Word travels fast among Indian people.

It seemed like Anderson had gotten real chummy with Emmett lately and they were acting like maybe they wanted to do some private talking. I figured it must've been that they wanted to get together and talk about rodeo tactics or something. But anyway since Emmett had gotten into this habit of where he was always staring at Bernadette in this kind of creepy way, and I could tell that him doing that made her nervous, she didn't put up any objection when I mentioned that me and her might enjoy going around with Mae and Henry and Tom and looking at the sights. I said that Anderson could catch up with us later on.

And so that's what we did, which accounts for how come we ended up getting so stuffed, since at every house we visited to meet some aunt or cousin of Mae's we were expected to have something to eat and did so as not to be considered rude.

It had got to be pretty late by the time we went back to Mae's house to get some rest since we had to start off early the next morning in order to make it to that rodeo in time for Anderson to get officially entered. And by the way, Anderson never did show back up that evening at all—him and Emmett Take Horse had gone off somewhere in Emmett's pickup and we didn't any of us know where they went. I do know that Bernadette was kind of worried about him, but Tom said not to get all upset, that his brother'd be ready to go bright and early in the morning if he knew what was good for him.

And sure enough there he was, dozing in the back of him and Tom's pickup with Chaco when we got ready to leave the next morning before it was even light outside.

Come to think of it, I never did know where Anderson spent that night or what happened to Emmett Take Horse since he wasn't around that next morning. And I don't think Anderson told Bernadette, either. But he must not have gotten much rest wherever he was because he just stayed in the back and slept almost all the way to Ganado. I sure didn't mind because at least that way I got to ride up front and see the country.

▼▼▼

Two men—one old and stooped, the other much younger—sat inside the eight-sided mud and log dwelling alone and hidden from the view of any passersby in the hills overlooking the Canyon de Chelly outside Chinle, Arizona.

There were no windows and so the air inside the one-room hogan was hot and stifling—almost suffocating—from the too-large fire that burned in its center on the hard-packed dirt floor. Too large a fire anyway for such a warm summer night. The heavy smell of smoke and of filth was overpowering. The bright, flickering orange light from the fire revealed that the room was not kept clean and tidy as was the custom among the Navajo people.

The old man sat wrapped in a heavy, ragged blanket, cross-legged and close to the fire. His stringy gray hair was tied back in the traditional way with yarn. Across his forehead, a dirty, purple scarf was knotted above his left ear. The old man's eyes were half-closed—they showed the milky white fog of near, if not total, blindness. And while there was no sound to be heard except for the low moan of wind across the smoke hole opening directly above the fire, he swayed slowly back and forth as though keeping time to some vague and distant drumbeat that only he could distinguish. When he finally spoke, it was in the old language.

"This thing that you come to me for, you know you gonna have to pay me big to get this kinda medicine?" he asked. The two sat in the old man's hogan—the younger man was a night visitor.

"You know I'm a big singer and that my father was a big singer too and that those peoples over there," he waved his filthy, wrinkled, old hand in the direction of the mouth of the canyon, toward the town of Chinle, "You know those peoples over there they say that my father did the bad side—that he chanted the Evilway and they tell how he would sit for a long time and just stare at

some person and then that person would eventually get sick and maybe she'd die or else that person's wife or her sheeps would die or something else terrible would happen to that person. *They say my father was a witch and that it was him who shot at that white preacher over to Lukachukai that time and caused him to not walk upright no more and they would have killed my father for sure, but he got knocked down by the lightning over there in that Canyon del Muerto before they got a chance and then he never got up again—even after that singer Slim Man did the Shootingway chant over him.*"

The old man leaned over, racked in a fit of coughing. He spit into the fire.

"*Way back that was, but my father, before she got killed, showed me first to do that way—to do the Nightway and them chants for Frenzyway and Moth Madness—how to make peoples get sick and to die.*" His voice cracked with age and what sounded like vile hatred. "*And I know how to do it and I can do it and those peoples over there they figured out I got something in my mind, but they're all scared of me and afraid to look directly at me.*"

The old man stretched out his hand and, feeling about, took hold of a piñon root knot from a jumbled pile of firewood behind him and placed it onto the already leaping flame of the fire. The sticky pine pitch from the knot caught quickly and the pungent heat in the room became even more unbearable. And yet the old man gathered his blanket still closer about his scrawny shoulders. Once more he hacked and coughed, and again he spit into the blazing fire.

"*I do have somethin' in my mind,*" the old man went on. "*I know how this witchery business is done. But just knowin' the right prayin' to do, it ain't all it takes neither—you gotta have some certain things to make* something bad happen," he said, becoming more and more agitated as he spoke. "First you gotta know the person you're aimin' to witch. You gotta know that person's secret name and sometimes that's hard to find out since even their family don't hardly ever call them by that name outside of their hogan. And then you gotta have somethin' private of theirs—like maybe some part of their clothes that ain't been washed or some of their hair or fingernails, or even some of their shit or somethin' that they spit out from their mouth."

The old man's eyes suddenly opened wide. His head turned slightly to where his gaze—if, indeed, those cloudy white eyes could be said to gaze—fell directly upon the face of his visitor.

"How do I know that you want to have this power bad enough?" he hissed. "If I'm gonna teach you these ways that my father taught me, I gotta have one big price."

The old man glared at the young man sitting across the fire, as though he were sizing him up.

"I got no use for sheeps or moneys," he said. "You want to know this Anit'in, this Witchery Way and how to get some of this here corpse poison, then you gonna have to show me you deserve that kinda power."

The filthy old man hitched his blanket once more around his shoulders and resumed swaying back and forth, his eyes again half-closed as he turned back toward the fire, his voice quieter now.

"You're gonna have to bring me some real strong witchin' medicine . . . somethin' from one of them chindi hogans over there in that village before I'll trust you with any more of this Witchery Way business."

Hearing that, the younger man was gripped with an almost overpowering fear. He felt the painful ringing in his ears return and he shivered in the stifling heat as though he'd been drenched in ice water. He struggled to catch his breath.

The old man spit into the fire. "That's the price of initiation you gotta pay to get into this business."

Just then a sudden gust of wind came down the smoke hole of the hogan—exploding sparks and heavy, acrid smoke from the piñon pitch fire filled the cluttered room.

Coughing and choking in the thick, black smoke, his eyes stinging from smoke and sweat and his vision blurred, the young man stood and stumbled awkwardly to the door and out into the near-total blackness of the warm Chinle night.

As he climbed into the battered, green pickup truck he'd left parked just outside the hogan, he could not see that the little black and gray dog that waited in the bed of the pickup was cowering far back near the tailgate—as far from where the driver sat as possible. Neither he nor the passenger who sat in the truck's cab could see that the dog was trembling violently—from some ancient, primal fear —and that the hair across its neck and shoulders stood and bristled. The pitch-black darkness and the low moan of the wind through the canyon below prevented both the young men from seeing that the dog's lips were drawn back —baring white teeth—and from hearing the low, mournful growl that came from deep in its throat.

The driver sat motionless, trying hard to control the fear that burned in his throat. Gathering himself, he turned the key and pumped the accelerator to start the engine. Switching on the parking lights, he could just see in the dim glow of the instrument panel that the one sitting beside him in the cab looked nervous . . . scared even.

"You can quit that worryin'," he said as he backed the truck away from the hogan and turned toward the paved road.

"This old man's got strong medicine—he's gonna help

us to get rid of them bad feelin's in your head."

Rubbing the back of his scarred hand across dry, cracked lips, Emmett Take Horse managed a half-smile to himself as he steered through the darkness down the two-tracked path that passed among the scrub oak and juniper. As the pickup drew near the paved road, he reached up and switched the lights back off, stopping for a moment to make certain no other vehicles were approaching that might see them coming out from this place. Once he was satisfied that the road was deserted, he turned the truck onto the pavement and sped toward the town of Chinle—switching on the bright headlights only after they were well down the highway.

"Gimme a sip of that hootch, bro." He reached a misshapen, three-fingered hand toward the bottle and, turning it up, took several gulps of the whiskey. Again, he wiped the hand across his mouth, sucking air between his teeth at the sour, hot burning in his throat. The fear had all but receded from his mind. He handed the bottle back to Anderson George.

"Take a swig of this good fire water," he said. "And quit actin' so fuckin' scared. The old man wants me to get him some of the stuff he'll be needin' to fix you up, that's all. It ain't you who has to go inside of that place."

Witchcraft is the most heinous of all Navaho crimes. The practice is not as uncommon as most people believe.

—Richard F. Van Valkenburgh
"Navaho Common Law II" (1937)

Starr

nderson really wasn't well. And I don't think it was just the booze that accounted for his condition, either. He had been tall and slim ever since I'd first seen him, but he got to where he looked downright skinny. His eyes were all sunken in and his cheeks looked hollow. I was concerned, and I know for a fact that Bernadette was nearly sick with worry.

I remember one afternoon she told me that she was sorry but that she wouldn't be able to come to the house for a couple of days since her family was making a trip to Arizona, to Chinle. I had a hunch that somehow the trip had to do with Anderson's problem and I asked Bernadette about it. She told me that they were going to see if a traditional Navajo medicine man could help in any way, and that they were going first to see Anderson's grandmother and that she was a "hand trembler."

I've read a lot about Indian medicine and know that the belief in things like hand tremblers and medicine men is common among the Navajo people. But I've also read that hand trembling is actually only a peculiar kind of seizure disorder to which Navajos attach supernatural significance—they believe that hand tremblers actually have the ability to divine things: to find lost items and to diagnose sickness. Diagnose ills, that is, but not cure them—that being the responsibility of a medicine man or singer. Apparently hand trembling is really just a minor seizure, whereas the more severe type of seizure—the kind we know as epilepsy—Navajos refer to as "moth madness." It seems that the Navajo sees a person in an epileptic seizure fall to the floor—often sees that person fall into the cooking fire in the middle of the hogan— and because he knows that a moth is attracted to flame and will fly straight into the flame, the Navajo understands this to mean that the person in an epileptic seizure and a moth flying into a flame are both afflicted with the same "madness."

Still, I couldn't help but think that Anderson needed to see a real doctor who could perhaps make him well and I'm afraid that I told Bernadette so—and I offered to pay for a trip to see someone in Albuquerque if it was a question of money.

You know, I really just wanted to help in some way. Bernadette was polite but she was also firm when she informed me that no white Albuquerque doctor could help with Anderson's sickness.

As it turned out, I suppose she was right.

▼▼▼

Hunched forward over the wheel, intently studying the wet sand ahead, Emmett Take Horse steered the battered, green pickup around what experience told him was a sink hole.

It was experience that enabled him to recognize how the soupy sand looked—to recognize the signs even by the glow of the headlights of a moving vehicle. Simply knowing the layout of the canyon floor wasn't enough. Quicksand, he knew, moves and shifts constantly. A place where one day you could stand on solid ground might, within a matter of hours, shift and broil to the point that the same place would bog a truck down to its axles or suck a good horse up to its belly inextricably.

Then, coming to the place he was looking for, he swerved and brought the truck to a sudden stop beside a stand of cottonwood and Russian olives.

He killed the engine and shut off the headlights. Leaning across the seat, he reached in and took the flashlight from the glovebox before opening the door and stepping down onto the damp, firm sand.

Standing for a moment beside the truck, adjusting to the darkness, he could just make out the dark shapes of the tall cottonwoods and the sheer rock wall of the canyon that loomed high above him. He pushed the switch on the flashlight.

As he hurried through the shadows shaped by the flickering light, Emmett Take Horse stumbled along the barely perceptible path, out of the clump of blue green olive trees and across the untended corn field. As he ascended the slight incline that rose up close to the base of the steep canyon wall, Emmett made straight for the dark shape that he knew to be the small mud and rock hogan.

Even though he knew this place—had passed by it on any number of occasions—he would never even have imagined stepping inside. And now, the thought that he was about to actually go into the place caused him to feel a near-intolerable fear. It was a horror that gripped him. His mouth was dry and his back drenched with sweat. He felt cold and he felt weak. Most of all, he was very much afraid.

Breathing heavily now, he stopped as he reached the entrance to the empty dwelling. Directing the yellow beam of the flashlight to the right side of the door, along the rough exterior wall, he turned and, walking slowly, followed the curved surface until he reached that place—as he'd known he would—where there was a gaping hole in the wall on the north side of the structure.

More even than a mere hole, all that remained of that side of the hogan was a pile of rubble.

It was as though someone had pushed in the wall at that place deliberately.

And, indeed, someone had pushed in that wall. Emmett Take Horse knew that this was a chindi place—a ghost hogan. An abandoned structure where some person had previously died and whose corpse had been removed, as Navajo tradition requires, not by way of the single east-facing door, but rather by knocking a hole through the north wall of the hogan.

For the Navajo, north is the direction of all evil.

Emmett Take Horse aimed the beam of his flashlight through the opening in the wall—into the center of the room where there stood a small iron cook stove. On the far side of the room he could see that a saddle was hanging by a piece of baling twine from the cribbed log ceiling—its leather cracked and dried, it was covered thick with dust.

Except for the dust and the piles of litter—the twigs, the scraps of wire and shiny tin, the bits of bright-colored cloth—except for those things left by pack rats in exchange for whatever treasures the rodents had been able to carry away, the inside of the hogan looked much as it had the day its occupant had died.

It was not surprising that nothing had been disturbed by human hands. No Navajo would dare to enter a place where someone had died. And white men—not particular if those they robbed were living or dead—were not allowed in this canyon unless accompanied by Navajo guides.

His breathing came faster and faster, his eyes followed the darting beam of light as he explored the room. He felt sick to his stomach—a bitter bile rose burning in his *throat. He felt as though he might pass out.*

Finally he found what it was he had been searching for. The light fell upon what remained of the pallet of dried and yellowed pine needles and grass where the occupant of this hogan would have made his bed . . . the place where that man would most likely have died.

Gathering himself and bending slightly, Emmett Take Horse stepped over the rubble and into the hogan. Reaching out, he steadied himself to keep from falling. He kicked away the dirt and dried grass from the pallet, it was real terror that he felt as he moved the light across the bedding, he was searching for something in particular. Kneeling down, he wedged the flashlight into a crack in the stone wall so that its light shown on the bed and began to brush and paw through the dust and the straw—frantically examining the small stones and pebbles and discarding each until he found exactly the right one.

In the palm of his trembling hand he held a smooth, thin river rock—round and thin it was, the size of a silver dollar. He turned the stone over in his hand . . . here was a stone that would not have caused a lump in the bed of a sleeping man—a stone that would not have been removed. Here rather, was a stone that would have gone unnoticed—one upon which a man would surely have slept.

More importantly, however, he held in his hand a stone upon which the corpse that had been removed from this place would almost certainly have lain.

Emmett Take Horse shuddered. He stood up in the damp darkness of the chindi hogan and placed the stone deep into the pocket of his jacket.

Grabbing the flashlight from where it was wedged in the rock wall, he turned to leave. He stumbled over the rubble in the north wall of the hogan, and fell hard to the ground. Pulling himself once more to his feet, Emmett Take Horse hurried away into the dark.

If you want to kill the man himself, they say . . . [the witch] can speak the secret name of the man he is after. The best way to do that, they say, is for the [witch] to sit on horseback, not moving at all, and watch his victim who can't see him.

—Clyde Kluckhohn
Navaho Witchcraft (1944)

Gracie

As it turned out there was only four other guys besides Anderson who'd signed up for the saddle bronc event at the Ganado rodeo, and three of them didn't stay on till they buzzed the buzzer and so didn't get no score. Anderson had what Tom called a fair to middlin' ride but still ended up winning, which I thought was pretty exciting, but which didn't win him but about eight-and-a-half dollars in prize money on account of the light turnout.

But even though Anderson hadn't won all that much money for coming in first place in the saddle bronc riding, him and Tom were so pleased with the whole thing that they said they figured we could afford to stay at least one night at a motel before we got all the way back home.

"There's this real well-known old hotel in Gallup with a big lobby and a swimming pool and its own restaurant where they fixed up all the rooms and put these signs with the names of famous movie stars on all the doors," Tom said. "It's supposed to mean that the movie star whose name is on the door stayed in that particular room sometime or other while they were making a movie somewhere close by or else passing through town—like on their way to Hollywood, California, or New York City."

Well, that sounded like exactly the kind of place where

me and Bernadette would love to stay and we said so. The guys didn't argue.

Right off the bat we started speculating on whose room we might get to stay in—I said I hoped we'd get somebody like that guy that plays the hero in all those *Rambo* movies but Bernadette was more in favor of Cybill Shepherd. Tom laughed real big at that and said that these were old time movie stars who'd stayed at this hotel back in the olden days and more than likely we'd wind up gettin' a room named after somebody we'd never even heard of like maybe somebody who had just a little part in some old black-and-white picture show. But I said never mind, I still thought it was gonna be exciting to stay in the same room where real live movie actors had stayed.

Tom said that the only room he wouldn't stay in even if it meant he'd have to sleep out in the truck with Chaco was if they had one named "The Ronald Reagan Room."

"Anybody foolish enough to say out loud that Indian people were gonna have to move off the reservations if they ever wanted to become American citizens, don't deserve to have no hotel room named after them, much less be a movie star and then get to be president of the United States," he said.

And none of us could argue about that, of course.

So even though it was one of my most favorite events to watch, I still couldn't hardly wait for the bull riding part of that Ganado rodeo to get finished with so we could get goin' for that hotel.

As soon as it was over with, Tom made Chaco jump up in the camper so he wouldn't make trouble for us and we walked over to the Hubbell's Trading Post, which is a pretty popular place. We browsed around and admired all the rugs and other stuff they had in there for a little while and then used their bathrooms before we went back and piled into the pickup for the ride over to Gallup.

I can tell you one thing, that Anderson was feeling pretty darn cocky about having won first place—for which I can't say that I blame him, either. But it seemed like the farther we got from the rodeo grounds, the better his winning ride got—at least the tellin' about that ride got better. And believe me, that Anderson did keep telling about it, too—over and over. Naturally Tom razzed his brother quite a bit . . . he wasn't about to let him forget about what all had happened back there in Piñon when that horse flipped over in the gate. But it was fun-type razzing and Anderson didn't get testy or anything. Like I said though, he was sure enough feeling cocky.

In order to go from Ganado to Gallup, you have to drive through Window Rock, which is still in Arizona. At least that's how we went. And since I'd only been at Window Rock one time before and that was when I was a lot younger, back even before our mother died, I was sort of hoping that we might get to stop at the Navajo Tribal Museum there which I remembered as being real interesting for a quick visit, but of course I didn't say anything about it and we didn't stop. It wasn't all that late, but Tom said he wanted to get on to Gallup in time to get us some good movie star rooms before the hotel got all filled up with tourists on their way to California from Oklahoma. And besides which, we were all getting pretty hungry and if we wanted to eat at a good cafeteria that him and Anderson knew about, Tom said we better get a move on. It's funny how even after all that good food that I'd eaten back at Hopi—added to which was all the hot dogs and pop and stuff you just naturally have at a rodeo—I could still be feelin' so hungry. But just thinking about goin' into a cafeteria made me start wondering about what all I would choose from that long line of different foods.

There's one more thing I ought to tell about that part of the trip, and this is something I thought was kind of creepy.

As we were driving through Window Rock—which isn't really a very big town even though it's the headquarters of the whole Navajo tribe—well, as we were driving through there we happened to pass this gas station and I remember I was looking out the side window scratching Chaco's ears and daydreaming to myself when I happened to notice this beat-up, old, green pickup sitting there in that gas station parking lot and that there was a guy in a black hat kind of leaning up against the side of that truck who was staring directly at us as we drove past. As we got even with him I recognized that it was Emmett Take Horse who it seemed to me like we kept seeing everywhere we went. The thing is, he wasn't putting gas in his truck or checking the oil or anything like that. He was just standing there watching us while we drove past—like he was waiting and had been expecting to see us. Bernadette and the guys in the front didn't notice him, I don't guess. Least ways they didn't honk or wave or anything, but just kept on driving.

But *I* saw him . . . and so did that dog Chaco.

▼▼▼

In case you hadn't noticed, I'll tell you that Tom George was quite a talker and he knew a whole lot about a lot of different things. So the rest of us weren't all that surprised when, as we were going down the road between Window Rock and Gallup, Tom fell to lecturing us about the place we were heading for.

The main street in Gallup, New Mexico, he said, is what used to be the main highway, except back then it was called Route 66. He said that nowadays the interstate passed by the outskirts of the town, but that old Route 66 had got famous for being the main road across America, which of course meant that practically anybody who ever went on a vacation or even a business trip to almost anywhere in the United States of America eventually wound up driving through Gallup, New Mexico. And even though Gallup isn't actually on Indian land, it is completely surrounded by Indian land—what they call a "border town." And even though you can't buy whiskey or wine or even beer on Indian land, you can buy that stuff inside the Gallup city limits. And you can also sell or at least pawn your turquoise and silver work. All of which just means that Gallup is where a lot of Indian people go to pawn their jewelry. It's sad to say, but that's the reason that just about the most that all them tourists who ever passed through Gallup ended up gettin' to see was this long line of hock shops and liquor stores and bars. That and of course the usual store-front missions and churches that just naturally appear wherever there happen to be a bunch of Indian people. Tom said lots of Navajos nowadays get fed up with the old ways—that they get tired of stayin' up all night doing traditional ceremonies and so end up joining the Holy Rollers that come around with their tents and hold revivals.

And on top of that, Gallup is also a place where one of the main railroad lines runs through the town. And Tom said that when you mix people and whiskey and trains together that it's usually people who come out the losers— that people sometimes manage to get their legs or even their heads cut off by passing locomotives.

Bernadette squealed and made a face whenever Tom said that, and told me not to pay any attention to him— that he was only kidding about the trains. But Anderson took up for Tom and swore that it was true and told us just to keep our eyes peeled and to count how many people we'd see in wheelchairs or on crutches with just one leg left.

To tell the truth, I don't know how true that story about the trains was, because I don't remember seeing anybody with just one leg or worse yet with no legs at all, but Tom sure was right about there being a lot of hock shops and bars. It was a lot worse than I'd ever seen in Dulce, or even in Farmington where as you know they have a *real* problem with alcoholism.

We did see a big tent though, all filled up with rows of folding chairs where they were fixin' to hold a Holy Rollers revival, it looked like. I don't know, I just think it's a real shame how those rich preachers are all the time hanging around reservations and trying to get ahold of what little money the Indians have in the first place.

▼▼▼

Steadying and turning the flat stone on the log stump set like a table before him, the old man clutched the knife in his withered hand.

His rheumy eyes squinted in the pale yellow light of the kerosene lamp as he worked slowly and methodically at scratching lines on the stone's smooth surface.

When he'd finished drawing the almost childlike stick image of a man, he handed the stone and the knife to the young man seated beside him.

Emmett Take Horse smiled as he scratched two words beneath the crude portrait:

Pretty Soldier

▼▼▼

I still remember how the white woman behind the counter at the hotel had her hair all done up in this big beehive-style and was wearing a long dress that looked a little too dressy to me for somebody who was just working as a desk clerk.

I mean, even the girls who work the desk at the brand new motel back home just wear clean bluejeans, or if it's the busy season they might sometimes wear skirts. I thought this woman might be the hostess in the restaurant who was maybe just filling in for the regular desk clerk who was sick or had to go to the dentist or something. Anyway, I also can remember how that woman looked over at me and Bernadette kind of suspicious-like while Anderson and Tom were arranging for the rooms.

The two of us girls were busy looking at all the framed pictures on the walls of old-timey movie stars—mostly they were the kind of stars who acted in cowboy pictures, plus there were a lot who didn't look too familiar to either of us. And we peeked in the door to the big gift shop where they had these gaudy signs stuck up everywhere that tell how all the Indian jewelry is "On Sale" at "50% Off" like it always is in those places out on the interstate that sell curios and exhibit live rattlesnakes and have Indian-sounding names but are really run by Jews or Arabs—I never can tell those kinds of people apart.

I swear, but that was one fancy hotel lobby. They had big overhead lights hanging down that were made out of old wagon wheels and there was big couches that you could sit on and wooden desks with lamps where I guess you could write postcards to send home to friends if you wanted to and deer heads with glass eyes were hanging on the wall over by the giant stone fireplace. And something I hadn't ever seen before, there was these chairs made out of cow horns! I swear they really were these great big horns that formed the back and the arm rests on these chairs!

But I guess the weirdest thing of all—to my mind, at least—was they had these two stuffed Indians that were sitting on their own chairs together over by one wall. Of course they weren't *real* Indians who'd been stuffed—it was more like they were these two big, life-sized dolls that had on Indian clothes and colorful headbands holding on these wigs that were braided in long pigtails like I guess

Indians are supposed to wear. Bernadette whispered to me that she believed white people sometimes had their pictures taken with these stuffed Indians so that when they got home from their vacation they could tell their friends that they sat next to a redskin. It was pretty funny, that's for sure.

When they finished checking in, Tom gave the woman cash money to pay for the two rooms at which point she started acting not quite so suspicious. I guess it's not too surprising that she would be kind of leery at first. A fancy hotel like that isn't used to getting a lot of Indian people staying in their expensive movie star rooms.

We ended up getting rooms on the second floor that were named after people none of us had ever heard of— not even Tom George. Me and Bernadette got one named after some man and the room that was assigned to Anderson and Tom said a woman's name—I remember it was *Marleen* or *Murleen* or something. Our rooms were right next to each other and we looked in them both and found out that there wasn't really much difference between them except for the color of the carpeting and the names on the doors. So Bernadette talked the guys into trading with us so that our room had the girl's name.

We brought our stuff along with Anderson's saddle up to the rooms and then we rode over to the cafeteria that the guys knew about to get us some dinner.

It was a Furr's Cafeteria and they had all my favorite things: they had steaks and fried chicken and mashed potatoes, and of course beans and fried okra which I just love but can't ever make it come out as good as cafeterias can whenever I try to fix it at home, and cornbread and rolls with real butter that comes wrapped up all neat in blue tinfoil, and pies and cakes and red jello for dessert. And just like at the cafeteria down in Albuquerque where

I ate once before there was this lady that came around and refilled your iced tea or coffee for free if you wanted some more. It was just real nice.

Tom George ate two pieces of pie, but I believe he was just showing off. Of course since he was paying for everything out of his pocket, he had a right to eat however much of anything he wanted to I'd say.

While we waited for Tom to finish eating his pie, we decided we were going to go back to our rooms and watch a color movie on the cable television, but then Anderson told us he wished we could take a walk past some of those hock shops on the main drag so that we could look at the stuff in the windows—he said that even though they have bars and steel grills over the fronts of those places at night to help keep the robbers out, he thought you could still see some of the stuff that they sell in there. So Tom found a place to park and we all went walking down that old Route 66. Chaco wasn't real happy about it, but he had to stay in the truck seeing as how the street was so busy and we were afraid he might get ran over.

We saw a lot of stuff like guitars and horns and type-writers and eight-track music tapes in the windows of the different stores, but there was also a lot of empty spaces that Tom told us was where they put out the valuable silver jewelry and rifles in the daylight, when they didn't get robbed quite so often. Then while we were walking past some of the bars we noticed that there would be all these drunks hanging around out front and they'd watch us as we walked past, but mostly they wouldn't say anything rude. Probably because they could tell that Tom and Anderson wouldn't likely take no guff.

We had done most of our window shopping and had just turned around and started to head back toward where we left the pickup and were passing for the second time this one real dark doorway where a couple of especially bad drunks were kind of leaning—one was kind of squatting, actually—when one of them started saying something to us.

"Hey there, brother."

We kept right on walking, of course, figuring it was just some drunk looking for spare change.

"*Hey you!* Hold on there, bro," the guy was real persistent. "Ain't that Anderson George I see walkin' there?"

Well, we sure enough stopped when we heard *that* and Anderson squinted his eyes and peered into the dark.

"Yeah," he said. "Who's that talkin'? Do I know you?"

"Shit, don't you recognize me?" The voice was slurred. "It's me—your old buddy Franklin . . . Franklin Charley."

I could barely see in the dark, but I could tell that the man who was talking was wearing this dirty, green army-type jacket and that it was torn pretty bad on one of the sleeves. This same guy was also trying to stand up and was having a hard time getting his balance. He tried to steady himself against the wall—he reached his hand out toward Anderson.

"Hey man, is that that brother of yours you got with you? . . . is that that sumbitch Tom George walkin' with you?"

Anderson stepped into the dark doorway.

"Franklin Charley," he said, taking the man's hand and pumping it up and down. "What the heck are you doin' here at Gallup? They told me you joined the army.

"Tom," Anderson said, "look at here, it's Franklin Charley—you remember Franklin, don't you?—the best goddamned bronc buster on the whole Rez."

Me and Bernadette stayed out on the sidewalk—in the brightness of the streetlight. We were glad that this drunk person was somebody that Anderson and Tom knew . . .

that there wasn't any trouble getting ready to happen—at least not as near as we could tell. But then, wasn't neither one of us too comfortable, either. The guys talked for a couple of minutes while me and Bernadette looked in a window of a western clothes store that happened to be right there. Then I could hear Tom talking to Anderson. His voice sounded kind of mad to me, and even a little bit nervous, I thought.

"We better not," he was saying. "Come on now, Anderson, let's get on back to the truck and get goin' before it gets too late. We gotta take Bernadette and Gracie back to their room now."

Then they got to talking too hushed and low for me to understand from where I was standing.

All the time that this was going on, Bernadette was getting more and more nervous and antsy and was sort of slowly inching her way up the street in the direction to where the truck was parked, and of course I was inching right along with her. It wasn't hard to tell she didn't like whatever it was that was going on one little bit, and neither did I.

I thought maybe I could get Tom and Anderson to come on with us.

"Hey, you guys," I said, and I said it pretty loud, too. "That cable movie's gonna be startin' in a couple of minutes and we don't want to miss the opening. Let's get goin'."

By this time, me and Bernadette were about halfway up the block. And then Tom came hurrying to catch up with us.

He was by himself.

"Come on," he said. "I'll drive you all up the street to the hotel and then I'll come back and get Anderson."

You could tell that Tom was kind of upset, and of course Bernadette wasn't exactly all smiles, either. Me, I was just feeling confused. When we got to where we had parked and Tom unlocked the door and we got in, I couldn't help from asking who was that drunk guy and how come it was that Anderson was staying back there with him instead of coming on with us.

"That was a guy that we used to know by the name of Franklin Charley," Bernadette said. "He was a couple of years ahead of me in school down in Santa Fe."

"Charley was a bronc rider—probably the best that there was back when we were doin' high school rodeos," Tom said. "Anderson used to hang around with him some and I guess he showed my brother quite a bit about contesting in rodeos.

"I never did have much use for him myself because it seemed like he was all the time sneakin' around, drinkin' and gettin' in trouble. Then as soon as graduation came he up and joined the army. I haven't seen him around since then, but it's easy to see the wine's got ahold of him now."

Thinking back now, I can't remember ever seeing Tom George look as worried as he did right at that minute. I didn't know what was worrying him so much.

After Tom let us out in front of the hotel, Bernadette and me went upstairs to our room and sat on the queen-sized bed and watched cable television.

I could tell that Bernadette wasn't all that interested in the movie even though it was in color and we got in at the very start of it, and she kept getting up and looking out the little peephole in the door every time she heard even the slightest little noise out in the hall.

After about two hours we got kind of startled when somebody started knocking on our door. Bernadette peeked out and then undid the little brass chain that's supposed to keep robbers out but don't look all that strong to me and opened up the door. I figured it was the guys and I was pretty relieved.

I was partly right. It was just Tom George, by which I mean he was by himself.

"Didn't you find Anderson?" Bernadette asked.

"Yeah, he was still at that same place. He's just havin' a visit with Franklin Charley," Tom said. "And Emmett Take Horse, he showed up, too. Don't worry none, Bernadette, Emmett wasn't drinkin' and he told me he'd stick with Anderson and bring him here after awhile."

You could tell by looking at Tom that he was not at all happy with the situation and that he was just trying to keep Bernadette from getting too worried.

"Do you mean that Anderson was drinking?" Bernadette asked.

"Hey, you know Anderson," Tom made a big effort to smile at her. "He's gotta have him a drink or two if there's anybody partying. Just beer, though—I talked to him private and he promised me he wouldn't get drunk."

At first Bernadette looked real sad at hearing that, but then she said she wasn't going to let any of that kind of business ruin our stay in a movie star hotel room. She talked Tom into going and getting some cold cokes and potato chips out of the machines downstairs in the lobby and then the three of us sat around watching television and eating snacks.

After awhile Tom said he had a good idea and he told us to wait here and got up and left.

In a few minutes me and Bernadette got about halfway startled again when we heard this commotion out on the little balcony outside our window and then somebody started making this sort of a tap-tap-tapping noise on the glass. It kind of scared me, but then I went over to the window and cupped my hands around my eyes and squinted and could see that it was just Tom and that he was motioning for me to open up the window and when I did, in popped that Chaco dog just big as you please—I swear his little stub of a tail was going about a hundred miles an hour. Of course we all of us got a big kick out of that and the more we made over him the more Chaco got excited. Finally, Bernadette had to scold him a little and tell him to lie down on a bathmat to make him calm down. He must have been real happy to get to come in though, and not have to spend the whole night by himself out in the truck, because he never did make a sound or cause any more commotion after that and stayed real still all night long as near as I could tell.

Oh man, that whole thing was quite an adventure all right. But to tell the truth I would have enjoyed that Gallup part of the trip a lot more if everybody hadn't been so mad or worried at Anderson for not coming back to the room.

The last thing I remember was watching this kind of crazy movie about this blond-haired girl who looked normal most of the time but who was really a mermaid and if she got the least bit wet she'd grow this ugly big fish tail. I must have fallen asleep before it was over though, because the next thing I knew it was getting light outside and I was waking up and when I looked over I saw that Tom George was gone and Bernadette was sitting there in front of the mirror brushing her hair.

Chaco was sitting right beside her watching every move she made like he usually did. One thing, she didn't look to me like she'd been asleep because her eyes were all red and bloodshot.

"Did Anderson come back?" I asked her.

"No."

"Well where in the world do you think he is, Bernadette? I thought Emmett Take Horse was gonna bring him over here—did Tom go to look for him?"

Bernadette said that Tom had went to his room to go to sleep and that Anderson knew where we were and she guessed he would come back whenever he felt good and ready. You know, she was trying to act nonchalant about it.

But she was worried, that's for sure.

▼▼▼

As it turned out Anderson didn't wind up getting good and ready to come back to the hotel until after we'd eaten us some breakfast in the restaurant downstairs and then got all our stuff together and were thinking about we would maybe have to leave without him.

He showed up all by himself just about the time we'd finished bringing the last of the stuff down from the rooms and were about getting ready to start off. Naturally Chaco saw him first and started leapin' up in the air and acting all excited and foolish.

Anderson didn't look too hot. For one thing, his clothes were all dirty and crumpled and for another thing he wasn't wearing his black hat like usual. And on top of that, if you ask me, he smelled terrible—kind of like the stale beer and vomit that you smell in those bad barrooms up in Farmington. Of course Chaco was the first one to notice that, too.

"How you doin'?" Tom asked his brother when he came walking up to where we were standing beside the pickup. The way he said it was kind of like nothing out of the ordinary was goin' on and that he just hadn't seen Anderson for awhile.

"Not too good," Anderson said.

"Well you sure as hell don't *look* too good, either," Tom said. And it wasn't till right then that he started talking more like he was pissed off at Anderson for not coming back to the room last night.

"Where've you been . . . and where in the heck are your boots?"

Anderson looked down at his feet like it was the first time he'd noticed that he was wearing only socks.

"I dunno," he said, kind of sheepish.

"I just know I woke up in the jail a while ago and some son of a bitch had stole my hat *and* my boots, Tom."

Like I said, Anderson looked awful.

"Well what were you in jail for?" Tom asked him.

"Just to get some sleep," he said. "I didn't do nothin' wrong. But Jesus, Tom . . . there must've been about a hundred Indians in there . . . all piled on top of each other . . . some of them pukin' and other ones all bloodied up from where they'd been cut up in fights or run over by cars or something."

Anderson looked pale now—like just remembering that filthy drunk tank was about to make him sick to his stomach.

"Is there somewhere in there where I can wash my hands and face?" he asked, nodding toward the hotel.

It was lucky for him that Tom hadn't turned in the keys to our rooms yet, so while Bernadette and I killed some time browsing through the half-price jewelry in the gift shop, Tom took Anderson back upstairs so that he could wash up and maybe get some of the smell of the Gallup drunk tank off him.

I should probably tell you that Anderson hadn't said a single word to Bernadette or me the whole time he'd been back—in fact, he hadn't even looked straight at either one of us. I figure he probably knew that my sister was not all that happy with him and more than likely he was more than a little bit ashamed of himself—for having ended up in jail, and for smelling so awful, and all.

◆

After a little while they came back down the stairs and I could see that Anderson looked some better since his hair was combed and tied back and Tom had gone out and got him his toothbrush and a cleaner shirt and some boots that must've been some extras from the back of the truck.

Still, Anderson didn't say nothing at all to me or to Bernadette but instead just went right straight outside to the parking lot and got in the truck and just sat there kind of moping and staring out at the cars that were driving past on Route 66.

It was then Tom told us that Anderson hadn't just lost his boots and hat, which would have been bad enough, but that he'd also been rolled of his billfold with all his money in it and that he didn't have no idea at all about what had happened that night before, or to Emmett Take Horse, either.

Later on I heard that they'd found Franklin Charley dead near the railroad tracks. By later on I don't mean later on that day, but that something had happened several months later. Anyway, it was wintertime, I know, because whoever it was that told me about what happened said that the cops had found him laying face down in an irrigation ditch and that he was frozen stiff as a board—it looked like he'd drowned in about a inch of water. They said he wasn't robbed or hit on the head or anything, but that he was dead drunk and had apparently been looking for some place warm to sleep and they figured out he'd fallen down and then just couldn't or else wouldn't get up. Now that was a case of somebody who just ruined his life with drinking, I'd say. Of course it wasn't all that unusual in Gallup. At least not in the winter.

When we hit the road I was in the back of the truck with Chaco, of course. But I could still tell that there wasn't a whole lot of talking going on up front the whole way home.

Bernadette was put out with Anderson, that's for sure, but she was also hurt by the fact that a good fun trip had been ruined—for her, at least.

I should also tell you that up until that time I hadn't never before seen what happened whenever Anderson got on one of his drinkin' spells. 'Course I didn't really see him drunk even then—just saw how sheepish and dirty he looked when he come up to us that morning after having spent the whole night in the Gallup jail. But I guess that was just a sample of what all went on—of what all Bernadette put up with from him later on down the line after they got married.

Bernadette didn't never complain, you understand— and she also didn't usually confide in me about what all went on, either. I believe it was because she was always hoping that something would happen to cause Anderson to give it up altogether . . . the drinking that is.

Later on I used to think back on that night and I always figured that the guys were probably driving through the rain and not talkin' hardly at all to each other. It made me sad to think that. You know, how probably Tom George was feeling put out with his brother for getting loaded and getting himself throwed in jail, and Anderson was feeling all sorry for himself on account of he was hung over pretty bad and because he'd lost his good hat and boots and also a bunch of money that he'd saved up for a rainy day.

But anyhow, at the time I could see that Tom was having a hard time getting over the fact that Anderson had managed to get himself drunk, and in Gallup of all places. And as if that wasn't bad enough, on top of it all some guys took advantage and rolled him and left him without a single dime to his name.

And I honestly wasn't sure Anderson was going to

make up with Bernadette either, since neither one of them two hadn't said six words to the other one for the whole drive from Gallup till we hit Shiprock. He spent nearly the whole time staring out the window and she occupied herself by fooling with the knobs on the radio or else studying her fingernails—studying her fingernails being something she'd always do whenever she was acting pouty or pretending to be mad at you. I say "pretending to be mad" because Bernadette wasn't one to ever really get mad about things—or at least if she did you wouldn't know it.

Then at Shiprock while Tom was putting gas in the truck and letting the dog take a leak and I was in using the restroom, they must've made up. Anyhow when we started back out on the last leg of the trip and headed for Dulce, I noticed that they were at least holdin' hands.

Tom saw that they were, too, and for the rest of the trip things pretty much eased up all the way around. Tom started back in talking and telling stories like always and even made a few half-hearted stabs at joking about Anderson's rodeo rides, like how his brother might could ride a sorry bucking horse and never lose his hat but let him spend a few hours in the Gallup jail and he'd lose his hat *and* his boots.

Anderson managed to laugh a little at that. But then he got real serious and started telling about a dream he'd had back at the drunk tank. It was like he couldn't get this particular dream out of his mind and it was upsetting him something awful.

"I was in this real deep hole or something . . . and the sides of the walls were very high up and so steep that I knew I couldn't get up there no matter what I did. And then it was like the hole was a gorge or a canyon and I was running as hard as I could and that place was getting narrower and narrower and I was more scared than I've ever

been. And then it came to me that I was running because
there was something following me. And I could hear
whatever it was back there and I could feel it. But I knew
for some reason that it wasn't really *chasing* me exactly,
just that it was followin' me. And then I came to this spot
where I could finally stop for a minute and get my breath,
and when I looked around I could see that there was
some broken piles of logs all in a jumble and a pile of rubble, and I was breathing hard—so hard that my chest
hurt. And when I turned around I noticed that the thing
that had been followin' me was a coyote and that it had
these bright yellow eyes and its tongue was hanging way
out and I could see its teeth and smell its terrible stinkin'
breath even. But just then it kind of disappeared behind a
bush . . . and when I looked around me again instead of
that pile of logs and stuff there was now in that spot a
hogan and our grandfather was standing there at the door
and I saw that he was motionin' for me to hurry up and
come inside. And I remember that he had a very worried
look on his face.

"And then I woke up. I was in that drunk tank and
the cops was bangin' on some big garbage cans and
telling all the drunks to get up off their lazy asses—that
it was time to get outta there and go home until next
weekend."

And you know, it's funny, but all the time that he was
listening to his brother tell that dream, Tom George
looked to me like he was very bothered by the whole
thing and I'd swear he turned real pale—I don't know,
maybe it was just because it was dark and rainy and he
was tired. Anyway, he told Anderson to just forget about
it.

"Them old dreams are just inside your head," he told
him. "Let's talk about something good for awhile."

So we spent the rest of the trip just recalling the dance

at Hopi and the clowns and all. I got sleepy and dozed awhile and had some dreams of my own, none of which I can remember so they must not have been too important. I know for a fact that dreams can sometimes be very important, but I couldn't understand why Anderson should act so upset over this particular dream. To me it didn't sound so awful. But I guess since Tom had seemed bothered by it, too, it must've been a Navajo thing—like maybe you're not supposed to dream about your grandparents, or something. It's hard to keep up with beliefs.

As soon as they took me and Bernadette up to our house at Dulce and helped us get our stuff inside, the guys immediately turned right around and hit the road again. They had to get on back to their jobs, and the gas drilling rig they were working on right at that time was clear down south of here.

I was glad to see that everybody was back to talking to one another again and that there didn't seem to be no serious hard feelings over the incident. For sure there ain't nobody who's perfect, and I was sorry that Anderson had got himself in trouble and that he was feeling sick and all, but he had to learn a lesson, didn't he? After all, it wasn't like anybody forced him to get drunk—I mean, he couldn't all the time count on his brother to watch out for him, could he?

▼▼▼

The rain was coming hard now—not falling down from the black sky in that way rain was supposed to fall, but rather blowing in torrents across the road: blown by the same strong gusts of wind that buffeted the black and silver pickup as if it were a toy. The sound was near deafening in its intensity: the rain pelting hard against the body of the truck, the thunder and lightning crashing, the wind howling.

Tom George tightened his already firm grip on the steering wheel and peered into the tunnel of light carved out of the blackness by the headlights—trying to see past the windshield wiper blades slapping ineffectively against the sheets of water cascading across and down the glass: the water now magnifying and reflecting the light . . . now dulling and blurring the darkness. The two-lane, asphalt road he drove was not straight and neither was it clearly marked—rather it had been laid out in seemingly haphazard twists and sharp turns as it wound its way among the huge boulders that lay broken and scattered as though thrown down by some angry trickster giant as it strode across this lonely stretch of Jicarilla Apache tribal lands. The pot-holed pavement rose and fell irregularly—rose up and then fell away according to the contours of the land. In the low spots there was apt to be water standing. In the darkness the standing water was especially hard to see and driving into that water, even at a moderate speed, was like stepping down hard on the brake pedal—a dangerous enough thing to do when the pavement was dry . . . a deadly thing to do in the rain. Or worse, there could be running water in those low places—places where the earth expected there to be a ditch or an arroyo to carry away the rain it could not hold. But the highway builders in their curious thrift and in their rush to complete the job decided not to make adequate allowance for the water—decided not to construct bridges over the small and normally dry arroyos—but chose rather to rely instead on flimsy culverts which, poorly maintained when they were maintained at all, were liable to wash out in the not uncommon thunderstorms that moved across this land. Yellow and black signs—inevitably riddled with bullet holes—warned drivers who could read to "Watch for Water," or "Do Not Enter When Flooded."

Tom George looked across the seat to where his brother

lay crumpled against the passenger-side door. How could anyone sleep through all this commotion, he thought. With the thunder booming and the rain pounding on the truck so? And Jesus, but the way this wind was shrieking . . . how could Anderson not hear this wind?

He's had a real bad day, Tom thought to himself. Tomorrow I got to talk to him about all this bad stuff that's gotten hold of him lately. For sure, it'll be a better day tomorrow and then I can tell him—make him see—that he's got to get himself straightened up.

In a bright flash of lightning Tom George caught a glimpse of what looked to be a car or perhaps a truck that had skidded or been driven off the road. He believed it was a pickup—in the flash of light it looked like it was an old and beat-up truck, and it seemed like it was probably green. But it didn't look like any kind of problem was going on, not like somebody was in trouble or anything. He'd just barely caught a glimpse of it, but he was sure the truck had been parked well off the shoulder of the roadway, close up against a cedar tree.

Tom didn't slow down.

After all, it wasn't unusual to see abandoned vehicles around this country, he thought. It seems like the cars Indians drive have a tendency to stop running a lot of the time . . . and usually at the worst times, too . . . like in a bad rain.

Tom realized then that he could hear the whining of the truck's tires on the asphalt—that the rain had let up all of a sudden and that even the wind was quiet now. These high desert thunderstorms can be locally severe, he thought, like the weather reports on the radio and the TV are always saying. It was as if he had driven over a line drawn across the road—a line where it was storming on one side and then barely even raining on the other. And just then, too, the road curved sharply around a massive rock the size of a large hogan. And as the truck's headlights swung in an arc across the darkness, he saw that there was something in the road ahead.

Tom leaned forward and strained to see—he eased his foot off the accelerator. *Goddamned livestock,* he thought. Or maybe it was somebody walking, some drunk trying to find his way home, or else somebody walking away from that abandoned pickup he'd passed back there.

And then the shadowy image ahead began to register fully in his brain, and Tom George saw—recognized, is more like it—that this thing in the road was not some animal crossing or some drunk staggering along the road. No, whatever it was, it was just standing there, perfectly still in the middle of the pavement. It was too big to be a goat . . . it looked wrong somehow, but still, he couldn't make it out. As he got closer Tom saw something that caused the blood to drain from his face and his mouth to go dry. He felt his skin crawl as he saw that this thing there in the road was a man . . . a man wrapped up in the skin of some animal. And he saw the head of the animal, whatever it was—a wolf maybe, or a large dog or coyote—was still attached to the skin wrapped around the man's shoulders.

Tom saw the reflection of the pickup's headlights flash yellow in its eyes . . . not in the man's eyes, but in those of the dead animal.

Then the man standing in the road raised his left arm and motioned for Tom to stop. Horrified by what he was seeing, Tom mashed his boot hard on the accelerator and swerved sharply to avoid striking the thing.

Just then Anderson George sat up.

The reflection from the lightly falling rain combined with the glare off the wet black asphalt of State Road 537 to multiply many times the effect of the pulsating blue strobes of the state trooper's patrol car and that of the flashing red lights atop the white Chevy Blazer bearing the Great Seal of the Jicarilla Apache Tribal Police.

Two men—one wearing a bright yellow rain slicker over the black and gray uniform of a New Mexico state trooper, the other the brown nylon windbreaker of a tribal policeman—stood side by side in the drizzle as they watched the attendants zip the wet body of the young Indian man into the large gray canvas bag and lift it heavily into the rear of the orange and white Emergency Medical Services ambulance.

The state trooper was Sonny Wiley.

"I suppose one or the other of us ought'a put that poor old girl back there out of her misery." He flipped his cigarette into the darkness. "What with it bein' a Indian cow and this bein' Indian land and all, I figure that'd be you, John." He fumbled under the slicker, searching for his spare pack of cigarettes. "Poor old thing is nearly dead already and just ain't got the sense to know it."

Tribal officer John Archuleta turned and looked toward the spot thirty yards up the road where, illuminated by the glaring spotlight directed on it from the patrol car, the dying Hereford cow stood trembling beside the pavement. Even from that distance Archuleta could see clearly that the cow's eyes were wide and glassy with pain and frightened confusion, and that a stream of frothy blood and slobber hung in a thick string from her muzzle to a black puddle on the ground. She stood there, oddly humpbacked and horrified-looking he thought, her three unbroken legs splayed out somewhat in an awkward effort to keep from falling—a fall from which she'd not be able to rise again, he knew. Her near hind leg—he could see that it had obviously shattered high, up near the point of her hip, when she was struck by the black and silver GMC pickup truck—simply hung there, bent out at a weird angle. The small red and white, clean-faced calf huddled shivering, wet and cold against its mother's warm side . . . tail drawn between its legs, the calf wasn't nursing now.

Archuleta handed his burning cigarette to the other man to light the new one he'd found and placed between his lips.

"That's one of Manny Foster's cows," he said. "I ought to try and get ahold of him . . . he'll need to bring his trailer and try and get her back over to his pens before she dies if he can. And he'll have to try and find a nursemaid mother cow for that little one."

"You gonna take the kid back to town with you?" Wiley asked. "He don't appear to be hurt none—just kind of shocky's all."

The two men looked to where the young man sat alone in the back seat of the idling Blazer. In the pale yellow glow of the dome light they could see that Anderson George was staring blankly after the flashing orange and red lights of the ambulance as it pulled away into the night.

"Yeah, I'll take him." Archuleta tossed his cigarette into the night. "Shit, you know I sure enough hate this part of it, Sonny. Seems like all there is to this goddamned job anymore is standin' around watchin' the ambulance guys pick up pieces of young people off the asphalt. If they ain't dead from car wrecks then they've blowed their brains out with a deer rifle."

He looked after the ambulance. "Them two George boys were about as close as any two brothers could be. This is bad, man . . . it's just real bad."

"You ask me, John, it's just another one of your typical reservation one-vehicle accidents. Official report always says pretty much the same thing: Subject has a couple of beers or a bottle of cheap wine, of course then you got your normal variety of livestock wanderin' around on the highway, it's drizzlin' rain and it's the middle of the night. Hell, seems like your people can always manage to find somethin' to run their trucks into out here in the middle of nowhere when they want to get themselves killed—if it ain't cows or sheep it's likely to be the only goddamned tree for a hundred miles.

"That, or else they find some seventeen-year-old kid lyin' dead in a puddle of water and have to chip his body outta the ice where he's froze to death overnight. Died from *exposure*, they say. Exposure my ass . . . sumbitch died from drinkin' rotgut Tokay is what he died from. Happens so often they refer to the stiffs as popsicles. Your Mexicans and coloreds, now they generally prefer shootin' each other with guns or cuttin' each other up with knives whenever *they* get tired of livin'—I'll be goddamned if it don't seem to me like Indians would rather kill themselves.

"George family live in Dulce?"

"No, they're not local. They're Navajos." Archuleta nodded toward the Blazer. "This one's got a girlfriend

lives up here, though. You probably know her daddy—
Edwin Lefthand? Drives a blue Ford."

Wiley shook his head. "Can't place the name."

"Eddie's a friend of mine. He married a Dulce girl and
moved over here from Taos, I dunno, fifteen, twenty years
ago. Married the youngest of the Iron Moccasin girls—
name was Theresa Iron Moccasin. She died several years
back . . . left him with two little daughters. Not so little
anymore, I guess—this guy Anderson goes with the older
one . . . real pretty girl name of Bernadette.

"I would of thought you'd know Eddie Lefthand for
sure—he's a foreman over at the new road maintenance
yard."

▼▼▼

*Thirty yards away from where the two policemen stood
talking, the dying mother cow turned her bewildered face
to nuzzle gently one last time the calf at her side.*

*She gave a low moan as a great shudder passed through
her body. Then the old cow's legs gave way and she fell
dead to the ground.*

When one ignores the prescriptions and the constant warnings from the Holy People which are relayed by Messenger Winds, or precipitates an imbalance by indulging in excesses, having improper contact with dangerous powers, or deliberately or unwittingly breaking other rules, conflict, disharmony, disorder, evil, sickness of the body and mind, ugliness, misfortune and/or disaster result.

—Charlotte J. Frisbie
Navajo Medicine Bundles or Jish
(1987)

Gracie

My sister and Anderson rode the train from over at Chama up to Durango and got married not more than six weeks after Tom George got killed in that freak accident.

Even though I never would have said it to her, as much as anything, I think Bernadette was worried that Anderson just couldn't stand not havin' Tom around. It was like he was completely lost without his brother bein' there. And while didn't anybody ever mention this kind of thing, it's a known fact that a lot higher percentage of Indians commit suicide when they feel like things ain't turnin' out good than do white people. I mean, all those social workers that get paid to hang around studyin' Indian people figured out a long time ago that suicides and pickup truck wrecks and alcoholism are the number one Indian killer. That means worse than regular diseases and asphyxiation caused from faulty butane stoves in the wintertime, even.

They did an official investigation of what all happened that night of the accident and according to what John Archuleta told my Daddy, they figured out that there wasn't any drugs or alcohol in Tom George's blood. That fact alone is enough to make it a freak accident. At least on this reservation it is. Of course wasn't none of us who knew him surprised to find out that Tom George wasn't stoned or drunk that night. We could've told them that without any investigation.

The problem with them getting married was, they did it at a justice of the peace up there at Durango and not in a normal church. All of which I can tell you really kind of tore our father up—what with him being pretty religious ever since our mother died added to the fact that he was Catholic, and all. But then he never could stay all that upset with Bernadette, and on top of which she sweet-talked him and said that the whole thing had been kind of what she called "spur-of-the-moment" and that her and Anderson had hooked up with some of their old friends from the Santa Fe Indian School who were living up there and attending classes at that college they got where if you're a Indian and know how to look pitiful you get to go for free. And she also told him that they'd had a real nice ceremony attended by people that they knew and who had known Tom George, too. All of which, I guess, was kind of important to them both. The icing on the cake was that she also told Daddy that they would do a traditional Indian wedding later on if he really wanted them to.

They never did, though.

What they did do was to come back down to Dulce and move into the second-hand trailer house that's parked out behind the cafe that Dee owns in town. That is, Dee owns the cafe and the trailer house. She said the place was just sitting there empty anyway and that it would be better to have somebody livin' in it to help watch out that it didn't get completely ripped off and that, on top of which shouldn't any young bride have to worry about where her house was gonna be. Of course, being that she was a business woman Dee naturally charged them rent every month, but it wasn't too much I don't think. Not when you figure both of them had jobs—which is kind of unusual around here—him at the gas drillers and Bernadette keeping house for the Stubbs.

Like most everybody else, Dee was just real fond of Bernadette. And at the time she didn't have no reason to dislike Anderson George, either.

Things went along okay—at the very first, anyhow. Naturally I missed having my sister at home, and I know that Daddy did, too. But Bernadette let on like she was happy living in that trailer with Anderson and she fixed the place up as cute as she could with curtains and framed pictures. Plus, Starr Stubbs gave Bernadette some expensive towels and, in addition, a color television set for a wedding present. Man, I would have thought that just those towels would have been a nice enough present, but a color television set, too . . . well, that was really nice.

And that wasn't all, of course. Dee from the cafe gave Bernadette some good dishes and John Archuleta and his wife gave them a crockpot for cooking in. And some of the girls who had worked with her over at the new motel went in together and got her this electric kitchen knife that you plug in the wall and it makes cutting up meat and especially turkey quite a bit easier. Me and Daddy bought some things for their house like dish soap and paper towels and cleaning supplies and light bulbs that we knew good and well they would need but never think to buy for themselves. So all in all Bernadette and Anderson were set up pretty good, I think.

▼▼▼

From where he sat at a booth beside the window of the motel coffee shop, Emmett Take Horse was able to see clearly when Anderson George paused briefly at the highway intersection before he turned toward the place outside town where his wife went every morning at this time to the job she had as a maid for the white people. He could see also that Bernadette sat beside her husband and that, as usual, that dog of theirs was in the back of the pickup.

He got up and went to the register and paid for his coffee. Then he walked out into the early morning air and climbed into his truck. He drove slowly to the trailer where Anderson and Bernadette lived and parked a hundred yards up the dirt road that passed behind it. He got out and walked quickly to the back door—keeping the trailer between him and the cafe in front. Although it was still too early for the white woman or her Indian husband to have opened the cafe/bar yet, he couldn't take a chance on them seeing him.

Just as he'd hoped it would be, the sliding glass door on the backside of the trailer was unlocked. He slipped quickly inside and went directly to the back bedroom.

For a brief moment he paused and looked about the room. He felt a sudden lightness in his head . . . the room smelled faintly sweet . . . it was her smell. He reached out and touched the bed where he knew she had so recently lain. Where he knew she had so recently lain with him.

Getting down on his hands and knees, he lifted the green spread and peered under the bed. He reached his good hand deep into the pocket of his coat and took out the flat stone. He had intended to place the stone on the carpeted floor beneath the bed, but instead—almost as an afterthought—he slid his hand between the mattress and the box springs. He withdrew his hand and replaced the bedspread. That was better, he thought . . . much better.

Sitting in the cab of the idling pickup in the parking lot of the recreation center, Emmett Take Horse was just lighting his third cigarette when he saw Anderson George drive past on his way toward the gas fields south of town.

▼▼▼

If things were going along okay at the first, they didn't
stay that way for long. I don't mean that there was any
trouble between Bernadette and Anderson, but it seemed
like he had really started going downhill ever since the
night of the wreck. I guess it got to where Anderson was
acting about half-crazy what with all the time thinking
that he had some terrible sickness and that he was fixin' to
die, even.

It's true that he wasn't sleeping or eating like regular
people, and for somebody who wasn't ever anything but
slim to begin with, he had lost a whole bunch of weight
in the past couple of months and his face was looking all
sunk in and awful considerin' that he'd always been such
a pretty boy. And Bernadette told me that he was having
ugly dreams whenever he did sleep and that he told her
he was sure that all his problems were on account of
somebody or other witchin' him. I guess he even told her
one time when he'd been drinking that he was scared
that it was somebody who had died that was coming back
to take him to the underworld on account of the dead
person being lonesome for some company. Of course it
didn't take a genius to figure out that he meant his
brother, even though he wouldn't never even say Tom's
name after the wreck happened. That's the Navajo way,
you know. They believe that saying the name of a dead
person will cause that person's ghost to come and pester
you. And it doesn't matter how friendly or affectionate
that person who died was before, either . . . all ghosts are
dangerous.

I mean, it was awful bad for Anderson sometimes.
Bernadette said he was suffering real pain, that it wasn't
just in his head.

Then finally, when Bernadette was getting to the
point where *she* was about half-crazy herself with worry

over Anderson, it was decided that they had to once and for all find out exactly what was causing all this stuff. I know this might be hard for some people to understand, especially non-Indian people, but they decided that it was time to consult *ndishniih*—which is a Navajo word that stands for "hand trembler." A hand trembler is a person who has the ability to tell what it is that's causing a person to be sick.

You got to understand, these kind of people aren't like singers exactly—that is, they don't usually have the power to cure the sickness, but rather they're able to tell you what the sickness is and then tell you what needs to be done to fix it. Also, you might want to know that hand tremblers are usually women. I did one time hear about a man who lived over by Two Grey Hills who some people said was a hand trembler, but that was the only one that I ever heard about although that doesn't mean there might not be others. Anyway, besides telling what all's wrong with you, hand tremblers can sometimes even tell you where something is that you've lost or that was maybe stolen from your house. But mainly the job of a hand trembler is to tell you what it is that's wrong with you when you're sick so that you can get the right kind of medicine. So that you can get the best kind of singer to come and do the proper kind of ceremony to make you better.

The way it works is this: A hand trembler goes into this kind of a trance and I guess sees a vision or something that tells them what's the matter. And the reason they're called "hand tremblers" in the first place is because that during this spell that they're in, one of their hands or even their whole arm will start to shake or maybe flop around . . . at least it will kind of tremble.

It sounds sort of peculiar—I mean, a lot of the old ways sound peculiar. But everybody I know of who's ever

seen one of them says that it works. I'm not sure if my
Daddy ever actually saw one before or not, but he says
that a long time ago the Apache people used to have
hand tremblers, too. But that like a lot of the old ways,
they forgot how to do it. Nowadays if you need to consult with a hand trembler, you're just gonna have to find
yourself a Navajo.

So as it turned out, Anderson's old grandmother—
who of course is a Navajo and who is that one that lives
over near Chinle that all of us went to visit that time on
the trip before the wreck—she's supposed to be a pretty
good hand trembler. I told you how Anderson's grandfather is a famous singer? Well, apparently a lot of times
Navajo singers and hand tremblers are attracted to each
other and wind up getting married. Anyway, that's what I
heard.

Most of the time in a case like this one you'd send for
a hand trembler to come to your place. But since
Anderson's grandparents were very old and their pickup
didn't always run that good, Anderson and Bernadette
figured that the best thing would be for them to go to
Chinle. Me and Daddy went along, too, because a person's family and relatives and friends always do go to
these things. That's just the way it is. Of course the two
of us went in Daddy's Ford rather than have everybody
crowd up into the one truck. Although my Daddy joked
that if we were all Navajo people that's exactly what we'd
have done. The joke bein' that Navajos can somehow always manage to get their whole family inside one pickup—usually they do it by makin' the old women and kids
ride in the back with the sheep and the dog, I might add.

By the way, my sister had told Starr Stubbs that we
were makin' the trip so that Starr wouldn't be expecting
her to show up to clean over there. Bernadette said that

Starr was real curious about why we were goin' and so she told her it was to get some help for Anderson's worrying and not being able to sleep and that the first thing that had to happen was we were going to consult with a hand trembler. Bernadette said that even though she knew Starr read a lot about Indian ways, she hadn't really expected for Starr to have even heard about the hand trembler part of the Navajo Way, but that she had and told Bernadette that she'd read in a book that hand tremblers were really just people who had fits and why didn't we just take Anderson to see a real doctor like they have down in Albuquerque.

Starr Stubbs was always real nice to me and I know that she was real fond of Bernadette and thought she was giving her good advice—but I swear her sayin' that stuff kind of made me mad. I mean, I never can understand how come white people think their way is the only way to do things. Indian people been around a whole lot longer than they have and as a matter of fact were probably even better off before white people brought in all their "modern ways," I'd say.

Oh well, like Anderson said when Bernadette was tellin' us about it, "Aw, who gives a shit, anyway."

To tell the truth, I figured there would be some kinda big to-do associated with this hand tremblin' business, like maybe an elaborate ceremony of some kind.

But no, what happened was right after we got to their place Anderson's grandmother spread a blanket on the ground between the sheep pens and where we parked the trucks and then her and Anderson sat down facin' each other while the rest of us stood around and watched what all was happening.

Which at first I gotta tell you wasn't all that much.

First, the two of them start in talking back and forth

and kind of chatting with each other real low like they're just visiting. Of course since they were speaking Navajo I couldn't have understood what they were saying if they'd been shouting at each other. Then after visiting a little while, the old lady starts to look like she's dozin' off—you know, like she's maybe fixin' to go to sleep. But then I notice that the fingers on her right hand are sort of moving and quivering like an old person's hands sometimes do all the time, except that I'd never noticed *her* hands do it, and to tell the truth ever since the first time Bernadette told me that this lady was a hand trembler I couldn't hardly keep my eyes off her hands. I mean, it got to where it was almost embarrassing, like when you stare at somebody who's got an affliction and you want to stop staring, and you try, but you can't.

Then what started out as barely what you'd call a quiver got stronger and faster until that hand of hers was really goin' to town and jerkin' around and she was holdin' it out there in front of her kind of in the general direction of Anderson's face. And all the time this is happening, Anderson's just sitting there with his head kind of bowed down and it looks to me like he's staring at this one particular spot on the blanket between him and his grandmother. The old woman, she's not looking at anything as far as I can tell, her eyes are still shut tight and her face is all screwed up and twisted and it looks like she's in pain or at least straining real hard.

And then, just like that, it stops. And that hand that's been doin' all the tremblin' drops down beside her and just lays there all still like it isn't even connected to her body anymore, and in her face she looks very tired for a minute. When her eyes finally *do* open up and she begins to talk to Anderson again, I'm wishing I could understand what all she's saying—but of course I can't.

The whole thing didn't take very long. Maybe twenty

minutes, and most of that time was taken up with them just talking to each other. The hand trembling part lasted just a couple of minutes, is all.

Anderson George never was the kind of person that is a big talker you know. At least not like his brother was. But after that session with his grandmother he was even more quiet than usual. Him and Bernadette went off and sat by themselves for a long time while Daddy and I ate some food and visited with the old people.

Or rather tried to visit, I should say. The old grandfather didn't speak any English, you remember, and he sure didn't speak the Apache or the Taos languages that my Daddy could talk in. So most of what you could call visiting was done with the grandmother translating things into English. One funny thing was that the grandfather would point at us and say a word that I can't remember now but that his wife told us was the Navajo word that meant Jicarilla Apache people. She said it translated into English as "long winter" and that Navajo people use that word because of the cold winters we have up north.

The funny part was, my Daddy said that the name the old man was saying was exactly the same as the word that was used in the Taos Pueblo language for Jicarillas, but that in the Taos language the word means "deer meat," and is the word they use because in the old days Jicarilla people would always bring deer meat to the Pueblo to trade for things they wanted.

Talk about your coincidence.

Later on, after Bernadette and Anderson got finished with their private business, they came walking over to where the rest of us were sitting around.

It was then that Bernadette explained what all the grandmother had told to Anderson:

The old lady had first off reminded her grandson that according to the Navajo way, even good people are surrounded by dangerous things all the time and you really have to watch out. She said he should never forget that there are certain things that you're not ever supposed to do—by which Bernadette said she meant things that are *taboo*, except that in Navajo the word they use is *bahadzid*, which if you was to say it in English, you'd be saying "dangerous to do." Like for example it's considered real dangerous to pester ghosts or to go near a deserted hogan since that probably is where somebody has died, or to touch anything that's been struck by lightning—like a tree, for another example. And of course there are hundreds of more things that a Navajo learns not to do when he's just a little kid. Part of the problem though, is that nowadays so many of the young people go off to away-school, like to Santa Fe, and while they're there they hang around with white people and Indians from other tribes who don't live in the same old ways and so they get to where they forget to watch out for certain things that are harmful.

She explained that the main job of the Navajo medicine man, or singer as they're usually called, is to control all those dangerous things that cause illness in people and to make them go away. Of course before he can do any good, the singer needs to know what the sick person did wrong in the first place so that he'll know what ceremony will cure him. Naturally, that's where this hand tremblin' business comes in on account of it's the hand trembler who can tell what it was that caused the person to get sick.

Which means that whenever Anderson's grandmother was hand trembling over him she was able to see what the problem was and then to decide what kind of curing ceremony would most likely make him well.

Bernadette said that during the hand trembling ceremony the old woman had found out that Anderson's
main problem was he had some demon or devil in him
that was causin' him to want to drink whiskey all the
time. She said that this bad thing had got into him way
back before he was even born and that it had something
to do with his father who was the hand trembler's son
and had moved away a long time back and nobody knew
where to. It was something about him havin' killed an
animal in the wrong way or something like that—I didn't
really get that part straight. But then, to add to the problem, she had also claimed that at some time Anderson
had happened to walk across a place where a snake had
been crawling. Now, I have to admit that I had a pretty
hard time believing that one. I mean, how can you watch
out for where you're walking close enough to know if a
snake has crawled there? But I guess there must be some
way that I don't know about.

Anyway, since now she knew what had caused all the
trouble and sickness that Anderson was feelin', she was
able to tell what would cure him of it. It was lucky that
what she decided he needed was a Devil Chasing
Ceremony—one that the old grandfather knew how to
do. I say it was lucky, because if it would've been some
kinda ceremony that he hadn't known how to do, then it
probably would have cost a whole lot to get some other
singer to come and do it. This was one of those cases of
it bein' a good thing there was a medicine man in the
family.

Bernadette said it was gonna take a couple of days for
the old man to gather up the stuff he needed and to get
everything prepared. I guess he had to get in touch with
some helpers, too. But just knowin' that something was
fixing to be done helped make everybody feel better, I
think. A lot of times these old sicknesses are only in your

head, I know. But that don't mean you don't feel just as sick.

Anyway, I know I felt a whole lot better—knowin' there was gonna be a ceremony for Anderson.

▼▼▼

There was no moon to be seen, yet all around the hogan the landscape fairly glowed as the clear night sky shone brilliant with the light from countless stars.

Still, the only light inside the hogan was that from the flickering orange glow of the cedar fire in the center of the single room. The old medicine man and his assistant were seated on sheepskins directly opposite the door, beyond the glowing fire. Before the two men, laid out neatly on a woven saddle blanket, was the jish—the paraphernalia of the medicine man's art: among them brightly colored parrot feathers and vials of pollen and small buckskin bundles that held mysterious things. This old man was widely known across the whole of the Navajo Reservation as a most powerful curer—a singer of the chants that chase away devils. His helper, a younger man, had traveled the many miles from Tuba City, near the Grand Canyon, to assist with this ceremony and would be paid handsomely—in money and in sheep.

Beside the medicine man, at his left hand, sat Anderson George. The object of the ceremony—the old man's patient—was also his grandson. Cross-legged the young man sat, straight-backed and tall. Anderson George was hatless, his shining black hair untied, hanging neatly loose and straight, a red and gray striped blanket was draped about his shoulders.

In the dead silence of the room—the only sound was the occasional sharp crack of the burning cedar—Bernadette George sat beside her husband. To insure the success of this traditional Navajo Sing, it was necessary that it be attended by members of the patient's family.

Next to Bernadette sat Anderson's grandmother, who was the wife of the medicine man. And beside the old woman sat Bernadette's sister, Gracie Lefthand. All three of the women wore blankets close wrapped over their heads and around their forms.

Directly across the fire from the women, at the assistant's right side, sat Bernadette and Gracie's father, Edwin Lefthand. And then there were two young men that Bernadette couldn't remember ever having seen before seated next to her father.

Soon the medicine man and his assistant began to shake their rattles and to sing. To Bernadette's ear, the weird chant was unmelodic—its rhythm monotonous and strange. At a barely perceptible signal from his grandfather, Anderson George stood up, allowing the blanket to fall from his shoulders to the dirt floor of the hogan. He stood naked but for a small loincloth—the glow from the fire revealed the young man's tall slender body to be sleek and muscular, there showed no indication of the terrible sickness that he felt inside.

Then Anderson slowly made two circles around the interior of the hogan—walking slightly bent in order not to scrape his head on the low ceiling near the wall. When he had completed the two circles, the young man returned to his position beside the old singer.

Bernadette watched as the medicine man repeatedly and gently touched her husband's body with sprigs of evergreen and yucca, all the while chanting in the same monotonous drone words that she could not understand. Then the two youths that she did not know stood and removed their clothing. With help from the singer's assistant, they then rubbed ashes over their bodies and stood before the medicine man who continued his chant while the assistant instructed the boys softly in Navajo and drew strange signs on their chests and faces with red and *yellow paints that had been prepared beforehand and placed in small clay dishes on the floor before them. The grandfather then presented each of the two with hawk and eagle feather brushes with which they then proceeded to lightly dust and brush Anderson George.*

The medicine man and his assistant continued to shake their rattles and chant while, with a great deal of animation and all the while uttering strange high-pitched, animal-like yips and low growls, the two boys brushed the devils from Anderson George's body and pantomimed chasing these bad spirits from the door of the hogan and out into the moonless night.

After a few minutes, the two returned and, in an excited-sounding and lengthy speech, announced to the old man that the devils that had plagued this good man had now been chased away to go and pester somebody else—somebody bad.

Then the boys dressed quickly and resumed their places in front of the glowing embers of the fire.

The Devil Chasing Ceremony was ended.

The sun had begun to rise over the hills to the east.

▼▼▼

Instead of gettin' better after the ceremony, though, Anderson George just stayed the same. He didn't get no sicker, but he didn't get no better either. And the worst thing was his attitude. It was like he knew in his heart that there wasn't anything could be done for him . . . like he knew he was doomed.

I dunno, maybe there's some kinds of devils that even a real good singer can't chase away.

As it got closer to the time for Bernadette to have the baby, she arranged with Starr Stubbs to have me go up and do some of the cleaning at the Stubbs' house two or three times a week.

I overheard Rounder tellin' Starr that the fact I only had to come part time whereas Bernadette was needed up there at least five days a week was just that much more evidence that Starr insisting on Bernadette comin' around so much was really just on account of her wantin' some company. Of course the way I see it, it shouldn't take no genius to figure that out.

But it wasn't long after she had Anthony before Bernadette was back up there workin' on her regular schedule. She never really let on, but I figure the reason she went back so soon was on account of the fact that Anderson wouldn't go to work most days—that he'd stay over at Dee's drinkin' beer till they closed down most nights and then sleep till noon and maybe he'd go work a little while with Starr Stubbs' horses in the afternoon and maybe he wouldn't.

On just what Starr paid Bernadette—even though it was pretty good compared to bein' a maid at the motel— I guess they were having a rough time making ends meet. By the way, whenever Anderson would work with Starr's horses and get paid for it, it seemed like he'd always manage to spend that money before Bernadette ever got to see it.

Of course Bernadette stood up for him and said Anderson was sick, but she wouldn't ever talk about it— talk about what was the matter with him, that is. It seemed like ever since Starr spoke up and gave her expert opinion on Indian medicine that time Bernadette told her that they'd decided Anderson was going to have to have hand trembling done over him—ever since then Bernadette didn't ever seem to confide much in anybody about whatever sickness it was that had Anderson down.

Starr

Even now it pains me to think back to the way things had gotten for Bernadette there at the end. Anderson never did get any better as a result of all the traditional Indian medicine that they tried, and things just got worse for Bernadette, as well. Life looked pretty hopeless as far as those two were concerned. I mean, here was this beautiful, intelligent woman living in this awful, rented trailer parked behind a bar with a baby, an out-of-work husband who was drinking way too much, and no real future to speak of that I could see. Everything just seemed so screwy to me—like maybe it was all really some giant misunderstanding or mistake.

I can still see her standing there in my kitchen that fall afternoon when she told me, rather casually I would say, that the trouble she and Anderson were having was on account of a *witch*. I guess you can imagine how I reacted to *that*. At first I laughed at the notion of such a crazy thing, and then, when I could see that Bernadette was obviously serious about what she'd said, I wanted to take her by the shoulders and shake her till her teeth rattled and scream at the top of my lungs for her to get *real* for God's sake . . . that she knew very well there was no such thing as a witch!

But I couldn't bring myself to tell her anything of the kind. I may not be the most sensitive person around, but even *I* knew better than to dismiss out-of-hand beliefs that, while they may have been totally far-fetched, clearly seemed reasonable to Bernadette. I mean, if I've learned anything living among these people, it's that they're no different from anyone else in the way they view what goes on in their world: We all look at everyday events in our lives in terms of our commonsense beliefs and knowledge. The thing I could never get straight, even after I'd spent a lot of time living around Indians, is that the commonsense beliefs and knowledge of Indian people don't match up with those of white folks. And believe me, I've tried to understand their superstitions—really I have.

After Bernadette died I read everything I could get my hands on—all the authorities: the sociologists, the ethnologists, the anthropologists—and I think I know now what it was that Bernadette must have believed. I know it, that is, in an intellectual sort of way. As hard as I try, I still can't believe a lot of these Indian ideas in my heart of hearts, but I've come to see that not being able to accept them is more a result of my own culture than of any unwillingness on my part to be open-minded.

Listen: There are people today who truly believe there are witches walking around. That's how Navajos, for instance, explain terrible things—explain away those things, that is, for which they can find no other, normal, explanation. Understand, these people do not believe that the witches among us are human beings, but rather that they are cruel and heartless monsters who only appear to be human. They believe that a true witch is totally outside the realm of humanity, that he or she is a nasty, amoral thing that senselessly and uncontrollably attacks and harms people—they believe that a witch is the very essence of *evil*.

It's too late, but I really think the most upsetting thing to me is knowing now that Bernadette very probably believed not only in witchcraft, but also in the notion that witches add years to their lives by living out the time that would otherwise have remained to their victims.

I can't understand how it is that otherwise intelligent and literate people living in this country and in this day and age can hold to such beliefs, but then maybe I'm not the best person to try and understand these things. I mean, I don't even understand how a telephone works, or a light bulb, much less a television.

What I *do* understand is that Bernadette Lefthand is dead, and that something unspeakably evil and ugly happened to her. And I know, too, that she must have been very frightened when she died. And knowing that is almost more than I can bear.

Gracie

The powwow on that Saturday night was being held as a benefit to raise money for the Head Start program that the kids who are too little to go to the Day School go to instead. I guess you could say Head Start is kind of like kindergarten, except that it's for disadvantaged people like Indians.

The posters scotchtaped up all over town—like on the glass doors at the grocery store and the cafe and the post office—announcing this particular powwow said that there was scheduled to be three different drum groups taking turns performing and that the headman dancer was a guy from Jemez that I'd seen before who's real good and the headwoman was scheduled to be this lady from Taos who, as it turned out, was a friend of Bernadette's. I thought it was great to see Bernadette acting excited about this dance since she'd been seemin' pretty down for quite a spell and I figured this might be just the thing she needed to cheer her up. To tell the truth, I remember around that time thinking my sister might be having some bad times with her husband Anderson, even though she never did actually tell me that. Also, because she hadn't danced in public since way before she had the baby, this was going to be just real special. Not that this was a traditional dance that was religious or a competition or anything—this was mainly just a social dance. But still, it was pretty big doin's . . . at least for Dulce, it was.

I fixed me a bowl of cereal while I watched one of those game shows on television and then as soon as it was over I rinsed out my bowl and put on my coat and walked down the road to Bernadette's trailer house.

Naturally that little Chaco dog ran up to greet me just as soon as he could tell who it was comin' up by the big mercury vapor light out in back of the cafe. He started in jumpin' way up in the air and acting all foolish and excited, like he hadn't seen me in a couple of years when it had really only been maybe about a few hours. I scratched his ears good for him to show that I missed him, too. I remember that I noticed Emmett Take Horse's green pickup parked by the trailer next to Anderson's truck, which wasn't all that unusual though.

It seemed to me like that guy Emmett had been hanging around with Anderson more and more lately. I got to admit I didn't much like him and I already told you how Chaco sure as heck didn't either. But I guess Bernadette must've felt sorry for him or something on account of she was always putting up with him hanging around and fixing him food and all. The problem was, whenever he was around the main thing him and Anderson did was to go off someplace or other and drink whiskey. They had to go off to do their drinkin' since Bernadette wouldn't allow any kind of beer or wine or anything like that to be in the house ever since the baby was born.

I remember Bernadette was wearing bluejeans and a sweat shirt and some tennis shoes when she opened the door to let me in. She was holding the baby propped up on her hip and I noticed that she had her hair pulled straight back in a pony tail that was tied with a piece of green yarn.

"Hi sister," she said. "I just been waitin' for you to get here to watch this Anthony guy so that I can get dressed up without him pesterin' me. You want a coke or some popcorn? The popcorn's left over from yesterday, but it's still okay. Anderson went over to Dee's Place with Emmett to have a beer. I'm not sure if those two're coming to the powwow or not . . . like usual Emmett already had quite a bit to drink before he even got here."

I took the baby from her and followed my sister down the hall and into the back bedroom. I sat on the big queen-sized bed and played with Anthony so he wouldn't be fussy and watched while Bernadette put on the dress that she'd made by hand instead of crocheting and knitting booties back while she was waiting to have the baby.

I swear that was some dress. It had taken her almost six months to finish, and that was with her working on it for part of nearly every day, too. It was made out of the softest and whitest buckskin that you've ever seen. Daddy liked to tell about how he shot that deer several years ago up near the border of Colorado and how his friend Sam Billy who lives over at Farmington took and tanned the hide in whatever special Indian way it is that makes it come out cream-colored—or, like in this case, almost white. And I tell you, the job that that Sam Billy did was just about perfect. Whenever the buckskin was cut up and then put together into the dress that Bernadette made there was only this one tiny little hole that you could see that he'd patched—Daddy said that hole was where the bullet from his rifle had gone into that deer. He liked to brag that that deer had been dead before it even hit the ground.

And this dress was just very delicate looking, too, except you'd be surprised at how heavy it was. One time right after she first finished making it, Bernadette told me how she carried it over and got on the scales that are at the store and that she figured out the dress weighed something like thirty-five pounds! Which like you can imagine is a lot to be carrying around—especially when you're dancing. One reason it was so heavy of course was on account of all the beadwork that it had on it. That, and then the tin jingles she'd added.

The yoke of that dress was completely covered with this real fine beadwork that was mostly a dark blue and extended from the neck to clear down both the arms. And I don't mean there was just a narrow strip of beads like you sometimes see either—Bernadette had made a band of solid blue beadwork about six or eight inches wide in which she had worked in these perfect red and yellow designs—you know, Indian designs like triangles and crosses . . . things like that. I knew Bernadette had learned to do beadwork as a sort of a hobby at away-school over in Santa Fe, but I still couldn't ever see how she'd managed to get to be so good at it.

And besides all the beadwork decoration, there was this long, narrow leather fringe along the bottom of the arms that ran clear down the seams on the sides of the dress and of course all around the bottom. And in some places some of the fringe had tin jingles connected on the ends. Jingles, you know, are those little bell-shaped pieces of tin—usually cut out from beer cans or pop cans—that look nice but also make this real delicate and pretty little noise when they brush up against each other . . . like when you dance or walk around.

And then there were some long, colorful ribbons that my sister had sewn onto the front and back of the dress at the chest level that hung down real pretty-like. Bernadette told me that she just barely tacked the ribbons on the dress so that she could change them whenever she wanted to for whatever color she happened to feel like wearing at the time. On this particular night I remember the ribbons on the dress were blue and red.

I helped Bernadette braid her hair and attach some narrow strips of white fur so that they hung down even farther than her real hair did—and her hair was pretty long all by itself you know. Then together we looked through her jewelry box and picked out some long red and black earrings that were made out of porcupine quills. And a choker with four rows made from these hollow pieces of bone and with beads strung on leather that I thought was real attractive. It was one of those chokers like what Plains tribes wear a lot.

And then Bernadette took a shoebox down from the top shelf in the closet and showed me this beautiful ceremonial peyote fan made with red and blue and yellow feathers that I didn't know she had. It's traditional that a person carry a fan when they dance.

My sister stood up then in the middle of that big bed and turned around and around while she modeled everything for me and Anthony.

"Oh, that dress looks so pretty," I told her. "Now I bet you're gonna wear them moccasins that you got from the Utes up there in Colorado, aren't you—the ones with all the fancy blue beadwork that will match your dress."

Bernadette stopped what she was doing and smiled down at me in that way she had—that way where she'd cock her head a little bit over to the side.

"I believe I just better give you those moccasins, Gracie," she said. "I know that they'll fit you and I bet they'll look especially pretty when you wear them."

"But those are your best ones," I said. I could feel that my face was getting hot—of course I was excited at the thought of getting those moccasins that I'd admired so much, but I was also embarrassed like maybe she thought I was hinting that I wanted her to give them to me.

Which I maybe did want her to, but I wouldn't never come right out and ask or hint at even.

"You've always liked them and I think if you had them you might dance more often. I'll wear them this one last time and then I'm giving them to you as a present."

"For *keeps?*" I said.

Even now I can still remember how she reached down then and touched my face real gentle. She was smiling at me and looked so beautiful that it nearly took my breath. But I can still see in my mind how in those dark eyes of hers there was this sad kind of a look that I just couldn't understand. I felt like crying and I didn't know if it was because I was so happy to be getting those special moccasins or because of that deep sadness in Bernadette's eyes.

"Yes, for keeps," she said.

When we were finally all ready to go, Bernadette searched through some drawers until she found a pen and a piece of notebook paper on which she wrote a note and stuck it up on the icebox with a little magnet that was shaped to look like a Happy Face.

The note was telling Anderson that we had went on over to the powwow. Then we bundled Anthony up real snug and I carried him and we walked the half-mile up the highway to the recreation center. Naturally Chaco followed us even though we hollered at him to try and make him stay home and Bernadette even threw some things at him and scolded him pretty gruff. He wouldn't have any of that business, though. We could tell that unless one of us was to go back and hook him up to his chain which was tied to the porch rail, he was comin' along and that was that.

"Okay, then," Bernadette told him, making her voice sound real strict. "But they won't let dogs inside and you're gonna have to hang around the door all night and you just remember how sometimes the young kids tease you." And she was just lecturing that dog and shaking her finger at him the whole time. "And I better not get any reports of you actin' up or snappin' at anybody either!"

It's so funny to me how that dog could always understand what Bernadette said to him—I mean he started grinning and jumping up in the air when she said that just like it was the best news he'd ever heard in his life. At least it looked to me like he was grinning.

When we got up to the gym door two ladies who were our aunts were sitting at a table just inside, charging everybody a dollar to come in and marking the back of your hand with a rubber stamp to show that you paid in case you wanted to leave and then come back in. These two were our mother's sisters and they both worked at the Day School. Ruth Iron Moccasin was a teacher there, and her sister, Myrtle, was the school nurse. They hadn't neither one of them ever gotten married or had any babies of their own, so they just acted like all the school children were their children and believe me, them two were always involved in things with the little kids.

They both of them stood up and gave big hugs to Bernadette and then to me and said how glad they were that we had decided to come. They bragged on Bernadette's new dress and said they were gonna stop selling tickets early and come watch just as soon as she danced, that it had been so long since they got to see their beautiful niece dance. And then naturally they made a big fuss over the baby.

"You timed it just right," Myrtle Iron Moccasin told us. "They haven't even had the Grand Entry yet and there's gonna be a drawing later on for some very nice prizes so you girls still got time to get your tickets."

"They're fifty cents each," Aunt Ruth said, "and you might be lucky and win some silver earrings or a pretty dance shawl with fringe on it. There's eight different prizes in all which means you get eight chances for each ticket you buy. The money we raise from the tickets is gonna be used for the little kids to take a trip to the zoo down at Albuquerque when the weather gets nice."

I took a dollar out of my pocket and said I wanted two tickets.

Ruth tore two mimeographed pieces of paper off a little book that had been made by stapling about a dozen of them together. She handed me the tickets and a ballpoint pen that had writing on it that was some kind of advertisement for the feedstore. It's funny how I can remember that so clear, isn't it?

"Now you just write your name on the big part with this pen and then tear off that little stub and put the part with your name on it in that shoebox," she said. "And be sure you don't lose that stub and don't go runnin' off before we hold the drawing, either."

The two women each got a quarter out of their purse and bought one ticket themselves on which they then wrote down on the line that asked for the name: *Mr. Anthony George.* Which I thought was nice of them to do.

Bernadette bought herself two tickets, too, and then we went inside and found us a couple of empty folding chairs that had been set up in a circle around the basketball court which was where the dancing was held.

For a minute there I bet you every eye in the whole place was on Bernadette when she took off her coat and we sat down to wait for the Grand Entry to be announced. The reason was, she had a reputation of always being the best dancer and there hadn't anybody had a chance to see her dance for about a year. Oh sure, she'd been to several of these local little powwows during that year—just to watch or to help keep track of the entries when it was a competition. But tonight she was all decked out in her best new outfit and it was clear to everybody that she had come to dance. Quite a few of the older people came up and shook hands and greeted us and made over Anthony and a couple of them were even polite and asked how was Anderson George. My sister told them that asked that he had some business to take care of but that he might be over later.

After awhile when everybody got organized and the drums showed up, the announcer called for all dancers to assemble down by the restrooms and the water fountain and as soon as they did they held the Grand Entry and posted the colors.

I sat and held Anthony and watched the doin's, but of course Bernadette was right out there among them. It was real impressive, too—people dressed up in their best outfits and showing off all fancy-like. It seemed like there hadn't been a powwow for quite a while and people were just itchin' to dance and visit. There was also the fact that the Head Start was a popular program and a lot of the people there either had kids enrolled or else showed up to show they supported it. But then, I still like to think that one other reason there was so many people was on account of they heard Bernadette was gonna dance.

I tell you, during the early part of that evening that sister of mine danced every dance they had except of course for those that were restricted to men only—dances like the Sneak Up and the War Dance.

And then a couple of times she sat down to catch her breath and fan herself like crazy she was so hot. And then she'd hold the baby and maybe have something cold to drink. On those times she made me get out there and dance. Of course I don't even try to dance fancy like she does—I only do the slow traditional steps.

Here's something that was pretty unusual to my mind—they had *six* specials that night. Like usual there was one each for the headman and the headwoman dancers and then for the head little boy and head little girl. In case you didn't know, those people usually come from other towns and even though it's a big honor to be asked to be the headman or whatever, it still costs money for gas and food if you got to travel a long way and so a special is how Indian people help raise some expense money. I'd say it's sort of like passing the hat in some ways. Then they held a special for the main Head Start teacher, Mrs. Marcus, who turned right around and gave the money she collected during her special right in to the zoo trip fund.

And then, to my surprise and I expect to everybody else's too, the announcer called for the Red Leaf Singers to play a special for Bernadette.

"I want us all to honor one of the prettiest and one of the nicest ladies there is, and also I might add, one of the best dancers that ever came from around here," he said. "I'm talkin' about Bernadette Lefthand . . . or I guess I'm supposed to say Bernadette *George*, since she's a married woman with a pretty little baby boy now."

There was clapping when he said that. "Friends," he went on, "I've announced a lot of different powwows in a lot of different places over the years, and during that time I've watched this young girl bring real honor to herself, to her family, to the town of Dulce, and to Indian people everywhere with her good nature, her good dancing, and of course with all that grace and beauty she displays. I know that we're all real happy to see her out there on the floor again, showin' us how dancin's supposed to be done, and I think we should let her know how much we've all been missin' her at these doin's."

Then he turned and spoke to the head singer of the Red Leaf Drum. "Okay Johnny, let's hear your guys do their best intertribal. *Red Leaf!* And Bernadette, you come on out here and lead off this dance."

Well, you never saw anything like what happened then. Everybody, and I do mean everybody in the place got up to dance and of course first to pass by and either shake my sister's hand or give her a big hug and at the same time put money into her hand before they went around and got in line to dance behind her. And because it's the thing to do when someone in your own family is being honored like that, I was right there beside her holding Anthony and at the same time making a kind of a sack with the bottom half of my dance shawl so that Bernadette could keep on putting that money people were giving her into the pocket that I'd made.

Oh, but Bernadette was smiling and speaking to every person who came up to her while at the same time she had these great big tears just streaming down her face. To tell you the truth, I had tears in my eyes, too. I was just so proud of her that night—so very proud that she was my sister.

When the special for Bernadette was over, Ruth and Myrtle Iron Moccasin helped to count up the money and divide it so that Bernadette could give part of it to the Red Leaf singers who had played for her special which was the custom. But as soon as she'd done that she went right on over to where the announcer's table was and told him that she wanted to donate the rest of that money—and it was over a hundred dollars, too—back to the children of the Head Start program. The announcer told everybody what she was doin' over his loudspeaker and then he bragged some more about what a wonderful person Bernadette was—which I figure everybody knew already.

◆

It was just a fun and very special evening and both of us and everybody else was having a real good time—at least as far as I could tell other people were. That is, they were up until the time when Anderson George and Emmett Take Horse showed up—drunk as skunks, and Anderson acting ugly toward Bernadette and causin' a ruckus that embarrassed me and upset my sister something awful.

It starts out with this kind of a commotion over by the entrance doors. It's loud enough that most of the people in the gym turn their heads to look and see what all's going on over there.

There hasn't been any trouble up to then what with John Archuleta standing over there all evening in his policeman's outfit checkin' things out and makin' sure there isn't any hanky-panky in the parking lot or people bringing in cans of beer, and seeing that none of the young kids are smoking inside the restrooms or anything. And wouldn't you know, it's just our luck that the very first sign of trouble would have to be when Anderson George and that Emmett Take Horse come walking in and right away Anderson starts off making a scene by first off refusing to pay his dollar and then telling Myrtle Iron Moccasin in a real loud, rude-sounding voice that he needs to talk to Bernadette a minute. Normally that wouldn't be any problem—coming inside to find somebody to give them a message or something, that is—but in this case anybody can see that Anderson George is looped and can't hardly even walk right and with his loud talking he's calling attention to himself so that everybody does see it right off the bat. Emmett looks kind of drunk, too, but at least he's standing way over to one side with his arms folded, keeping his mouth shut and just watching. And to add to the commotion, the minute Anderson comes in the door, that dog Chaco, who's up till then been the perfect "hang-around-the-door dog"—waiting patiently outdoors all evening like he was told to—comes scootin' inside and takes right off across that gym floor looking for Bernadette in among all the dancers.

The next thing I know, Bernadette has come over and is right there beside my chair tellin' me to watch the baby while she goes over to see what it is Anderson wants. And she does—she goes over and stands there talking to him. You can tell she's trying to get him to keep his voice down and from where I'm sitting she looks small and pretty in her white buckskin dress and those blue moccasins. And Anderson, he looks tall and agitated for some reason. Even from clear across the room you can see that his face is all twisted up and dark and that there's mud on his boots and dirt on his shiny black and red nylon rodeo jacket like as if he's been working on the pickup or maybe falling down—which I figured in his condition falling down was most likely what happened.

I can tell that a lot of the people in the place are watching what's goin' on over there by the door and every once in a while I notice somebody glancing over at me to see what I'm doing and it makes me feel embarrassed like I wish I was someplace else. Their voices are beginning to get louder by now and even though I can't make out what they're saying, it's pretty plain that there's a big fight going on and I think maybe I'm not the only one in the room that's embarrassed. Then Bernadette turns away from him and comes walking back across to where I'm sitting holding Anthony. As she's coming over though, I see that her head is bowed down and that she's watching her feet while she walks—that she's not walking with her head up high like she usually does.

"Where's my coat?" She looks pale, like all the blood has drained down out of her face and she's fixing to start crying. Her hands are shaking and I'm scared.

I guess she can see that I'm scared. "It's okay, Anderson just wants some money." She's talking low so that only I can hear her. "I told him that I only have two dollars but he's acting ugly and doesn't believe me. Do you have any money, Gracie? So I don't have to go over and get him some at the trailer?"

I give her the three dollars and some change that I have in my pocket. "You're not gonna leave with him, are you?" I say. "You better just stay here, Bernadette. I'm worried that Anderson's actin' all crazy."

That terrible sad look is in her eyes again. "Don't worry baby sister—he's just been drinking and can't help acting that way."

Bernadette reaches out and touches my face and smiles—like she'd done earlier that evening. "Really now, Gracie honey . . . I promise you that everything's okay. I'll give him this money and then I'll be right back and we can enjoy the rest of the dance.

"Maybe if I can just remind him about that time he got that twenty dollars at that powwow at Taos . . . you remember that time, don't you, Gracie? What a good dancer he was that night? Maybe he'll stick around and dance if I remind him of that," her voice sounded funny to me—kind of desperate or something.

"Or maybe if he'd just go over and ask them in a nice way those Porcupine Singers would let him sit in with them and play their drum . . . you remember what a good singer Anderson was, don't you, Gracie? I haven't heard him sing in such a long, long time—wouldn't it be nice to hear him sing one more time, Gracie?"

And oh God, I was just feelin' so bad for her—hearing her say these things . . . I could feel these big old tears starting to come into my eyes.

And then she stands up and starts walking back over to where Anderson is there leaning up against the wall, his hands in his pockets, glaring over toward where we're talking. And I notice also that Emmett Take Horse is now squattin' down over by a big trash can smoking a cigarette and kind of grinning to himself. The way he looks gives me the creeps.

And just then—while my sister's still walking back across the gym—the announcer says over the loudspeaker, "Okay now, everybody get ready for the big drawing. Find your lucky numbers 'cause it'll be comin' up right after Porcupine Singers give us an intertribal. So let's all you folks out there quit bein' so lazy—everybody get up and dance! That means you, too, Bernadette! Where you think you're goin'? It's not even eleven o'clock yet!"

But Bernadette, she keeps walking on over to where Anderson is standing and then I can see that she gives him that money. They stand there talkin' low to each other for a minute or two and then that Emmett stands up from where he's squattin' down over there and goes up and says something to Anderson. Even from clear across the gym I can see that Bernadette is saying something to Anderson and reaches out and touches his arm like she's trying to get his attention, but he just turns around and both him and Emmett leave.

Oh yeah, and while all this is goin' on John Archuleta had got two young boys to sneak up and capture Chaco and make him go outside again.

▼▼▼

Emmett Take Horse turned off the highway and steered the pickup close to the window at the side of the bar and honked the horn twice.

In a few moments a ghostlike face appeared at the fogged-over little window and the glass slid open a couple of inches. A cigarette dangled from the face as it peered across the cold night air and into the cab of the truck. It studied for a moment the two young men who sat there before it spoke around the cigarette. "What'll it be?"

Emmett rolled the window part way down and spoke to the face. "Gimme two bottles of whatever's the cheapest wine you got."

The face looked disgusted. "It's you boys' stomachs you're fuckin' up—I just sell the stuff. I figure the cheapest I got's Garden Deluxe and you're in luck 'cause GD's the special this evenin' for only a buck-ninety each. That'll be four American dollars for two includin' the governor's cut."

The two young men sat drinking in the cab of the pickup parked to the unlighted side of the Big Valley Inn. The truck's engine idled roughly—the blower on the heater whined steadily.

"Man, your old lady's lookin' good tonight." Emmett Take Horse lit another in a chain of cigarettes. "But you shouldn't oughta let her go out to them dances without you like that . . . next thing you know, she'll be takin' up with some young 'pache dude and you'll be left holdin' nothin' but your limp dick."

Anderson took another long drink of the too-sweet red wine. His eyes were bloodshot and watery—it was obvious that he was having difficulty focusing his vision. And he had reached that point where he'd begun to lose all eye-hand coordination . . . in taking the drink from the bottle, he'd banged his front teeth sharply. He reached his hand to his mouth to check and see if he'd chipped a tooth. He hadn't.

When he spoke, his speech was slurred. "Hey! Don't you be talkin' any of your trash about my woman like that, goddammit. Bernadette's a hell of a dancer—best one around here and that's for sure—and she spends ever day workin' up there and ever evenin' takin' care of me and my son." Draining the last of the wine, he belched and wiped his mouth on his jacket sleeve. "She by God deserves to get outta that trailer house ever once in a while, don't she?"

Anderson rolled down the passenger window and tossed the empty green bottle back into the bed of the truck.

Emmett Take Horse laughed at Anderson. "I dunno, looked to me like you's givin' her some shit yourself back there, bro," he said. "I'm just sayin' if you don't take care of business, somebody else will, that's all—like maybe even me."

Anderson George had leaned across the seat in an attempt to better focus his gaze on Emmett Take Horse. This time when he spoke there was real anger in his voice. "And she ain't interested in takin' up with nobody either, you asshole—not with no Apaches and least of all not with some crippled up ugly little cocksucker like you. And don't you forget it, either!"

Emmett Take Horse could feel the heat of rage slowly rising in his face. No sonofabitch was going to get away with calling him a cripple—not even a drunk Indian was going to get away with that. He took a sip of the wine he held between his knees—he'd barely made a dent in the quart-sized bottle's contents. He passed the nearly full, green jug across to Anderson, who immediately turned it up to his lips and drank long and deep before holding it out unsteadily in return.

"No, man . . . you go on and finish it," Emmett told him. "After all, you're a big shot rodeo star with two good legs and a good lookin' wife. You drink it . . . drink it all down."

Emmett Take Horse smiled to himself as he watched Anderson George tilt the bottle up and gulp the cheap wine—smiled as he saw the sweet red liquid dribble from out of the corners of his mouth and stream down his chin, run in small rivulets down his neck . . . into his shirt *collar and onto the front of his jacket.*

That's right, Emmett thought. Drink it all . . . yes sir,
you're one big fuckin' Indian cowboy, all right.

▼▼▼

We didn't win anything in the drawing.

Bernadette came pretty close though, when one of her
tickets was just three numbers away from winning a free
permanent for her hair from Lucy's Beauty Shoppe. Of
course Bernadette wouldn't never get a permanent in her
hair, but I figure if she would have won she might have let
me use it.

It was getting pretty close to one in the morning when
I started to getting so sleepy that I couldn't hardly hold
my eyes open anymore. Anthony had been sound asleep
for a long time, of course, but my sister was still going
strong.

Powwows sometimes last until the sun comes up, or at
least until three or four o'clock in the morning. Mostly it
depends on the drummers—you know, how much energy
they have and if everybody seems to be having a good
time. And except for that little scene with Anderson, I
guess Bernadette was having a real good time.

Anyway, after the business with the drawing was over,
Ruth and Myrtle Iron Moccasin had come over and got
some seats next to where ours were. They took turns
holding Anthony—one would hold him while the other
one would get up and dance. They also had treated us to
a late night snack of Frito pies and cokes which was good
since Bernadette had given Anderson all our money.
When they noticed how sleepy I was getting they teased
me a little about not being able to keep up with two old
ladies, but then they offered to give me a ride to my
house in their car since they lived nearby. I was worried
that if I left Bernadette would have to sit down because
of Anthony, but then Ruth also insisted that they were

gonna take their little boy as they called him home with them for the rest of the night. They had lots of times baby-sat with Anthony whenever Bernadette needed them to—like when I got a chance to fill in as a waitress at the new motel that time—so they were used to keeping him.

They giggled and said it had been a good long while since they had a good lookin' gentleman to stay overnight at their house.

To be honest, I was kind of surprised at the time that Bernadette agreed to them taking Anthony to their place for the whole night. I realize now that she didn't really want to take him home to the trailer in case Anderson was there and wanting to argue some more.

I didn't want to look like a party-pooper and I told them I wasn't all that tired, but they just laughed at me. Bernadette said she wanted me to go on and get some sleep and to tell the truth, that was just what I wanted, too—except that I was worried about Bernadette and I told her so.

"Come on and spend the night at home," I told her. "There's no reason to put up with any more of that whiskey foolishness tonight."

"I told you everything's okay, sister," she smiled at me. "If I know him, Anderson's sound asleep by now. And besides, he's my husband. He wouldn't ever do anything mean to me, even when he's drinkin'—I told you he just can't help himself, Gracie, that's all."

I thought at the time that she was being too nice—that didn't nobody, and especially not Anderson George, deserve to have such a sweet person for a wife.

I couldn't help from feeling sad at the thought of leaving her there that night—of leaving her alone. I know I had this peculiar feeling in my stomach—it was like I had a feeling that something real dreadful was fixing to happen.

So me and Ruth and Myrtle gathered up all our stuff and made sure that Anthony was bundled up snug. Bernadette gave us all hugs and kissed her baby good night.

I don't think I'm ever gonna lose the picture I have in my head of how beautiful my sister looked as she stood there in that white dress and waved good-bye to us at the glass doors at the recreation center.

It was clear and icy cold outside. Whenever I let my breath out it made puffs of smoke it was so cold. Chaco was still waiting and naturally he started leaping up in the air just as soon as he saw that it was me who was comin' out the doors. It was for sure he was ready to go home, too. But he looked all confused and anxious when he realized that neither one of the women walking with me was Bernadette, and then as soon as it dawned on him that she was still inside—that she wasn't coming out after all—he went back over to the side of the building and laid back down in the spot where he'd been waiting out of the way ever since they threw him outside.

And then as we were walking toward Ruth and Myrtle's Plymouth, I heard the drums start up playing again and I turned around and saw that Bernadette was still standing there just inside the doors. When she saw I was looking at her she smiled at me and then she pointed down at those blue beaded moccasins she was wearing and then pointed toward me to remind me I guess that those moccasins were fixing to be mine. Not that I needed reminding.

Just then some girl tapped her on the shoulder and she turned around and even from that long of a ways off I could tell she was laughing when she went back into the dance. I felt okay right then because at least she seemed like she was havin' a real good time.

I loved my sister so much. I was hoping things would work out for her—hoping things would work out between her and Anderson.

But that was the last time I ever saw Bernadette.

▼▼▼

Now she was aware that her right foot was bare and that it felt so very cold.

Aware that she'd somehow lost one moccasin as she'd fought against what was happening to her early on. Early on, that is, before she'd simply let go—before she'd given in to this dreadful thing that was happening . . . this thing that she couldn't understand.

And now she was thinking about the beautiful new dress she wore—about how it had been ruined as she lay there on the frozen mud beside the trash barrels. As she lay there in a widening pool of blood that was at first warm and sticky but that soon clotted and turned black, she thought about how the clean, white buckskin of the new dress had been ruined by that blood and by the trash and the dirt there on the ground. Ruined by the blood and the filth and the rips and cuts.

Funny, but she didn't feel any pain, and she wondered at that. She could remember seeing his face clearly—how it was dark and twisted in ugly rage and what looked to her to be fear, even. Why should he be afraid? And she could remember seeing clearly too the knife in his hand and she remembered how she'd tried so desperately to cover herself as he slashed wildly, again and again at her face and her body. And she remembered hearing the faraway sound of a woman screaming . . . and then realizing that it was she who was screaming. And she wondered at how the screaming had stopped so abruptly and how the sound of the screaming had became a choking sound . . . a bubbling and a gurgling sound.

She remembered how she'd looked down once to see

steam rising off the sickeningly sweet-smelling blood that covered her hands and arms and flowed thick and black from the long gashes across the front of her dress and how she'd felt only surprise and curiosity where her mind told her she should have felt pain and horror. But it seemed as though this terrible thing were happening to someone else—certainly not to her. It was as if she were standing outside herself—as if she were watching . . . watching a jerky, out-of-focus motion picture . . . a motion picture not in color, but rather in some old and grainy black and white.

Except that some things she saw were in color. Most of the blood was black, but some of it was red . . . some of it was very red.

And then she thought about her baby . . . and even though she tried hard, she couldn't remember where she'd left him and she wanted badly to look around her to see if he was somewhere there beside her but she couldn't lift her head . . . she couldn't move her head at all. Only with great effort and concentration could she move her eyes.

She felt so tired . . . she struggled with all her might just to keep her eyes open. She wanted to see things, but even more she wanted to rest . . . to go to sleep.

And then she remembered the dog . . . remembered seeing it snapping and biting frantically at his legs, and him kicking at it and cursing and finally reaching down to grab it by the scruff of its neck and lifting it struggling and shrieking into the air. How he'd ripped and torn the blade of the knife across its throat and belly and how she'd cringed to see it.

Remembered hearing the gurgling sound—the sound not of her own breathing this time, but the sound of the dog's breathing. Remembered hearing that awful sound for a time—remembered trying to figure if it was her or the dog—and wondering why it had suddenly become quiet again.

She was afraid and alone, but at least she was not so terribly cold now.

And then she thought about her mother. Thought about how, when she was a little girl, her mother had gotten sick and gone away to the Indian hospital and how she'd never come back home from that place. And she thought if only she could go home again it would make everything all right . . . that she'd be well again. She thought that the worst thing in the world would be to not go home.

She was just so very tired.

Struggling to keep her eyes open in the still, frigid darkness she was barely able to make out the dim outline of an odd-shaped object there on the ground a few feet in front of where she lay. With a concentrated effort, she focused her eyes on the shape and studied it for several long minutes.

For the first time since this terrible thing had begun happening to her, she felt tears beginning to well up in her eyes as she recognized that there on the ground before her lay her moccasin.

▼▼▼

It was nearly dawn when the two teenaged boys walked down the asphalt road that passed alongside the town park on their way home from the powwow. The two had been drinking all night outside the recreation center and were passing a last bottle of beer back and forth between them.

Hearing the sound of a vehicle approaching from behind, the one boy instinctively hid the bottle inside his wool-lined denim jacket while the other turned and stuck his thumb out in an appeal for a ride.

As it sped past them, both boys raised their middle

fingers in the direction of the battered, green pickup truck and its lone occupant.

"Asshole!"

The boy who held the beer drained the last of the flat-tasting liquid from the bottle and, looking about him in the dim morning light, spotted the vague outline of the trash barrel across the ditch in the park. He tapped his companion on the shoulder and gestured with his chin toward the barrel.

"Two points," he said. And he drew back and threw the bottle in a high, lazy arc.

The brown glass shattered as the beer bottle hit the hard frozen earth beside her head.

Sharp bits of glass fell into her hair and over the blue gray form that lay motionless beside her bare right foot.

Brushed lightly with the early morning frost, the little dog's pink and blue intestines stuck frozen to the earth where they'd spilled out of his body.

And although her eyes were open, they were fixed, unseeing, on that spot a few feet away where there lay the blue beaded moccasin she'd gotten from the Utes.

It was clear from the dull gray color of what but hours before had been shining black eyes, and the fact that there were tears and blood frozen to her face, that Bernadette Lefthand was dead.

▼▼▼

The light from the bathroom shown through the open door and fell across the bed.

Emmett Take Horse could see that Anderson George hadn't moved at all. Dead-drunk and passed out from the wine and whiskey, he lay sprawled face-down . . . exactly where he'd left him a couple of hours before.

He worked quickly then. Using cold water from the

bathroom faucet, he washed every trace of blood from his hands and face. He leaned across the sink toward the large mirror that covered the wall and examined his image carefully. He started to wipe the blood-smeared sink clean with toilet paper but decided against it—Anderson was too drunk to have thought of doing that. Then he sat on the side of the tub and removed the high boots—Anderson's boots—from his feet. In the bright light of the bathroom he could plainly see the marks where the blue dog's teeth had tried to tear into the flesh of his calves—where in one place they had very nearly punctured the thick cowhide leather. He was smart to have taken Anderson's boots—he had thought only to disguise his footprints with the larger-sized boots, but his own low-cut ropers would never have stood up against the little dog's attack. And he could see also where the boots were splattered with blood . . . as were the sleeves of the red nylon jacket with the black cuffs and collar—it, too, was Anderson's. His own coat was still on the seat of the pickup. His own boots lay on the carpet beside the sliding glass doors through which he'd entered.

Looking in again at the bed where Anderson lay sleeping—lay unconscious, really—Emmett Take Horse placed one of the boots and the blood-splattered jacket on the floor beneath the place where Anderson's foot dangled over the edge. He intentionally left the other boot there in the hallway. After all, he thought, a crazy drunk wouldn't undress neatly—a crazy drunk wouldn't undress at all . . . he might take off his boots and hat . . . maybe his jacket.

Especially someone drunk enough or crazy enough to have just cut up his own wife and dog with his hunting knife.

Emmett reached up and switched off the light in the bathroom. Then, pulling on his own boots he turned slowly and made a final check of the dark trailer before slipping through the glass doors and walking quickly out to the pickup truck.

Turning the key to start the still-warm engine and pulling out the switch for the headlights, Emmett remembered the bloody hunting knife there on the floorboard beside the accelerator pedal. He leaned down and picked it up and got out of the truck and went back inside the trailer. He walked quietly once more to the back bedroom and gently laid the knife on the bed beside Anderson George.

As he steered the battered, green pickup out onto the blacktop highway and headed west out of town, the cold, gray morning sky behind him was just beginning to glow in the reddish light of dawn.

He reached across and switched on the truck's radio. The early morning disc jockey for the Navajo Nation radio station whose powerful nighttime signal reached from Window Rock, Arizona, over the mountains and into the valley had just finished playing a Navajo language commercial for a Gallup pickup truck dealership. The voice sounded vaguely like that of an evangelical radio preacher in its slick-hick tones and forced enthusiasm:

"All right friends, it's just a few minutes now before Miss Selena comes waltzin' in here to tell you the latest news and then takes over and lets me go home to the wife and kiddies. So in the time we got left what say we change the pace a little bit. I don't know about you folks out there, but I kinda feel like hearin' somethin' from my main man. Oh yes, friends, you know I'm talkin' 'bout the old Rounder man himself. . . ."

Emmett smiled as he drove past the entrance to the rodeo grounds.

"Let's give a listen to Jim Bob Stubbs doin' a number

off his just-released album, Custer Had It Comin'. *Earlier we heard a cut from this new record with the Rounder doin' 'Geronimo's Cadillac'—now let's take a listen to his rendition of a fine old tune Johnny Cash used to do back in the . . . oh, I think it was probably the early sixties—not that I'm old enough to remember clear back then you understand. Anyhow, accordin' to the jacket notes, this here number tells the story of a Pima Indian boy who was one of the marines who helped raise the American flag up on Iwo Jima back in World War II . . . seems he became pretty famous for that until he got back home to the reservation and found out that not a whole lot had changed just because he was a war hero. Sound kinda familiar to you veterans out there, does it?*

"Anyway, this is dedicated to all the brothers out there in radioland who had the high honor and distinct pleasure of visitin' beautiful Viet Nam and who are maybe just now comin' home to mama from a hot Saturday night of, shall we say, indulgin' maybe a little too much in the grape . . . I want you all to remember what happened to this guy and take heed, you hear me?

"This here's Rounder Stubbs and his White Trash band with what I predict is gonna be a big hit out here on the Big Rez, this here is 'The Ballad of Ira Hayes'. . . ."

Emmett tapped one scarred and bent finger on the steering wheel as he hummed along to the sound of the radio.

Lighting a cigarette, he reached out and adjusted the heater control on the dashboard . . . the air was cold and damp. Up ahead, in the mountains toward Pagosa Springs, he could see that there was rain falling . . . morning rain, he thought.

Emmett Take Horse smiled broadly now as he pressed the accelerator pedal slightly and looked straight ahead.

As the truck passed the town park and the two hitch-
hikers, the road curved north. He could see that there
was lightning flashing in the canyon ahead. Strange that
there should be lightning, he thought . . . strange that it
should be lightning at this time of year . . . as cold as it
was.

The song about the drunken Indian was over now, and
the jarring voice of the pre-dawn disk jockey was replaced
by the softer voice of a woman who spoke briefly in
Navajo and then in English:

"Good morning, I'm Selena Manychildren and this is
First News of the Navajo Nation. . . ."

Emmett stubbed out a half-smoked cigarette, coughed,
and immediately lit another.

"Topping the news this Sunday morning, Tribal
Chairman Peter McDonald told a gathering of his
supporters yesterday at the Lukachukai chapter house
that he intends to plead not guilty to charges that he
accepted . . ."

▼▼▼

I know that a lot of young girls around here have babies
they have to take care of—that it ain't especially unusual,
even.

But I feel a whole lot older than most girls my age.

Listen, I love Anthony and I take real good care of
him. It's hard on my Daddy, though—bein' around that
baby all the time . . . at least the times when he's not at
work or over at the cafe visitin' with his friend Benjamin.
The way I see it Anthony is something very special that
Bernadette left for us—he's a part of her, you know. It's
just that I don't think Daddy can hardly even look at that
baby without seein' the part that's Anderson, and that's
what just about tears him up sometimes.

And another thing . . . not havin' a real mother or father is always gonna be hard on him, too, I expect. Hard

on Anthony, that is.

Lately I been thinkin' that it might be better if I was to take him and move far away to someplace else—to someplace like California, maybe.

At least California's one place where most people wouldn't know anything about how his real mother got murdered, and how when they arrested his very own father for havin' killed her and took him to jail that he told them he didn't remember doin' nothin' on account of he was so drunk that night. And how when they were questioning him they showed him some awful Polaroid pictures of my sister after she was already dead to try to get him to remember and to tell them what all had happened out there that night—how they say when he saw those pictures he got nearly crazy and started in banging his head on the wall and screamin' and actin' wild.

And then how on that next morning, Monday morning, when they went to his jail cell to take him some coffee and oatmeal that they discovered he had somehow taken and tore one leg of his bluejeans into strips and made a kind of a rope—and how he'd managed to stand up and balance on the sink that was in there while he tied one end around this pipe that was stickin' out from up by the ceiling and the other end he tied around his own neck—and how when John Archuleta looked into that cell he saw that Anderson George was hangin' from that pipe—hangin' there not wearin' nothing but his shirt and underwear—and that he was dead—and his tongue was all swollen up and black and his eyes were bulgin' clear out.

I hate to leave my home almost as bad as anything I can think of, that's for sure. But I don't know what else to do. Dee says you can get government checks in the mail out in California, and that the checks are for enough money to get by on if you're careful—especially if you have a little child and don't have no husband who can get a job.

I feel like my whole life is just about over with. Like it's already gone past me.

And I'm just barely sixteen.

A diffuse supernatural sanction against witches exists in the form of a belief that a witch who escapes human detection will nevertheless eventually be struck down by lightning.

—Clyde Kluckhohn
Navaho Witchcraft (1944)

▼▼▼▼▼

Acknowledgments

I am grateful for the support and encouragement of family and friends: Glenn Wiley, Renée Gregorio, Larry L. King, David Mair, Annie Hansen, Judith Bronner, Robert Murray Davis, and Noel Parsons.

Too, I am indebted to those good people who, although it is unlikely they are even remotely aware of their contributions, provided me with much inspiration in the telling of *Bernadette*: foremost among them, Lupita Trujillo, Virginia Dooley, Juanita Marcus Turley, Selena Manychildren, Nancy Wood, Carl Gorman, Luci Tapahonso, and Justin Tso.

And always there was Lefty, fine friend and constant companion. He was, quite simply, the best of dogs, and I miss him terribly.

Finally, grateful acknowledgment is made to the following for permission to reprint previously published material: The quotation from *The Navaho* by Clyde Kluckhohn and Dorothea Leighton, Cambridge, Mass: Harvard University Press, copyright © 1946 by the President and Fellows of Harvard College, renewed 1974 by Florence Kluckhohn Taylor and Dorothea Leighton, reprinted by permission of the publishers; the quotation from *Witchcraft in the Southwest*, by Marc Simmons, is reprinted by permission of the University of Nebraska Press, copyright © 1974 by Marc Simmons; the quotation from Charlotte J. Frisbie, *Navajo Medicine Bundles or Jish*, copyright © 1987, is used by permission of The University of New Mexico Press; the quotation from Richard F. Van Valkenburgh appears courtesy of the Museum of Northern Arizona Press; and quotations from Clyde Kluckhohn, *Navaho Witchcraft*, copyright © 1944 by the President and Fellows of Harvard College, are reprinted by permission of Beacon Press.

About the Author

Ron Querry, a descendant of the Sixtown Clan of the Choctaw Nation (Oklahoneli), is a member by blood of the Choctaw tribe. The author of three previous books and a member of the Native Writers Circle of the Americas, he holds a Ph.D. in American Studies from the University of New Mexico. Querry has taught at universities in Oklahoma, New Mexico, and Ohio as well as at the Penitentiary of New Mexico. He has worked variously as a ranch hand and wrangler, horse trainer and farrier, served as a racing official, and edited a national quarter horse racing publication. Querry makes his home in Tucson, Arizona.

THE RED CRANE LITERATURE SERIES

Dancing to Pay the Light Bill:
Essays on New Mexico and the Southwest by Jim Sagel

Death in the Rain, a novel by Ruth Almog

The Death of Bernadette Lefthand,
a novel by Ron Querry

Stay Awhile: A New Mexico Sojourn,
essays by Toby Smith

This Dancing Ground of Sky:
The Selected Poetry of Peggy Pond Church
by Peggy Pond Church

Working in the Dark: Reflections of a Poet of the Barrio,
writings by Jimmy Santiago Baca

▼▼▼▼▼